SALLY AT SCHOOL

BY
ETHEL TALBOT

THOMAS NELSON AND SONS, Ltd.
LONDON, EDINBURGH, NEW YORK
TORONTO, AND PARIS

THOMAS NELSON AND SONS LTD
Parkside Works Edinburgh 9
3 Henrietta Street London WC2
312 Flinders Street Melbourne C1
91–93 Wellington Street West   Toronto 1

THOMAS NELSON AND SONS
385 Madison Avenue New York 17

SOCIÉTÉ FRANÇAISE D'ÉDITIONS NELSON
25 rue Henri Barbusse Paris Ve

CONTENTS

SALLY AT SCHOOL

CHAPTER I

ENTER SALLY

"HOW *dared* he!" Sally drew herself up. She stood erect and sparkle-eyed. There was a hint of righteous indignation, too, about the sparkle in her eye which surely, under the circumstances, thought poor Grandmamma, ought not to be there!

"My dear!" she quavered uncertainly.

"There he goes *again*, upsetting you!" Sally's voice sounded that of a champion of the oppressed instead of that of a damsel whose grandmother had just been trying, very ineffectually, to administer the scolding which surely was well deserved. "He ought to be *sacked*. And if it was *India*——"

"My dear!" Grandmamma drew herself up at this. Here was something she *could* work from. "My dearest Sally, India is *not* England.

Indian native servants are *not* English servants. And to compare Rymer——"

" Almost a sound of reverence in your voice, isn't there, darling, when you speak of Rymer," interrupted Sally, taking no notice of her grandmother's impressive tone. " ' East is east, and west is west, and never the twain shall meet,' eh ? Is *that* what you're trying to say, darling ? " Sally's voice took on a protecting sound. " But all the same," continued she, striding along the lawn in her riding-breeches and coat by her grandmother's side, " I jolly well wish they *could* meet. Lots of the native servants would knock spots off Rymer—in good temper anyway." She stopped. " And, as for telling tales—" The scorn in Sally's voice grew terrible. She tapped her boots with her riding-whip and meditated, as though more in sorrow than anger.

" My dear child ! " Grandmamma's voice grew almost querulous. " Tales ! What an idea ! If I may not know, my child, what goes on in my own *house* ! And for a pony to be ridden up the front *stairs* ! And my beautiful piece of Old Lowestoft to be broken, as Rymer tells me, beyond repair ! "

There was a quiver in Granny's voice. Sally felt more and more furious with Rymer.

" And it would have been there still, unbroken and as hideous as ever — for I *do* think it was hideous—but for *him!* What did he want to come peering out of his cupboard for? I made *sure* he'd be downstairs at that time. What did he mean by boo-ing, too? *That's* what he did—*booed.* Did he think he was at a circus? Do you wonder that Puck backed? It was a wonder the darling didn't fall."

" Rymer said," Mrs. Heath spoke tearfully, " that the pony shied at the sight of itself in the glass, Sally."

" He didn't, then. So there. Rymer's a loonie, or worse. He *loved* seeing himself in the mirror. I was just explaining about how it was he and me we were looking at, and out came Rymer. It was the noise he made that made Puck back. And he'd even have backed beautifully—for, after all, I'd *meant* him to back down the stairs, and I was looking after him. If it hadn't been for Rymer, he'd *never* have broken the Lowestoft. Oh, *dear!* " Sally's voice for the first time expressed regret. " He's only managed the first flight, and I'd quite meant him to try the second to-day. Rymer's spoilt it all. I howled to him as soon as I'd got Puck quiet again, not to tell you. But off he went. The most disobedient——"

" He was quite right, my dear," said

Rymer's mistress with dignity. " If he had not——"

" If he had *not* you'd have had an utterly ripping birthday surprise that you won't get now, that's all," said Sally sadly. " For Puck's nerve's gone. I've been training him for weeks, and we'd never have had this setback but for Rymer. He was to have come in— right into your bedroom on your birthday, Granny darling—Puck was. It's all for *you* I've been doing it. He was to have brought you a bunch of flowers. He'd have loved doing it, the darling. And so would you have loved it, too. Well, and now that's off! I'm not going to spend hours and hours and hours——"

" Sally, Sally, it seems to me, darling, that you've too *many* hours on your hands," remarked her grandmother sadly, as they reached the house.

Rymer came to meet them. He had been awaiting them with features in which sorrow and anger seemed to mingle, and with hands filled to overflowing with portions of broken china. The butler deigned no look at Sally, the culprit ; his words were addressed markedly to his mistress's ear.

" Hafter hall these years, ma'am, for *this* to 'appen," he began sentimentally.

" Sentimental " was, at least, the adjective which Sally thought fit to use to herself ; she uttered the monosyllable " *Pooh !* " very loudly, and felt bored. After all, as she remembered with relief, Puck was intact ; a little shaken in the nerves, perhaps, but the pony might have been injured in his hurried descent down the drawing-room stairs.

She reminded Grandmamma of this in rather stately and comforting tones, then she retreated stablewards, leaving Rymer's old head bent deferentially towards that of his mistress while the pair consulted over the damage. She herself was thinking of her grandmother's last remark.

" ' Too many hours to myself ! ' Well, I *have*. Granny's owned to it at last, and I'll keep her to it." Sally, even during her brief visit to the stable, was making up plans for the next step in her campaign.

" Got an apple, Joe ? " half-thoughtfully she addressed the groom. " Yes, one of those Ribstons. Puck likes those best. Here, my beauty-boy ; eat it up, my precious. Oh, why *did* you buck ? You might have known I wouldn't fail you on those stairs." Sally's arms were round the pony's neck.

" 'E didn't break the mirror, did 'e, Miss Sally ? " Joe, the groom, was anxious to hear.

As yet only a half-tale from the kitchen quarters had reached him.

"Not he, the beauty. He only stepped into a big Old Lowestoft pot. It's unlucky to break mirrors, Puck darling, and you wouldn't have done it, would you? Suppose it should be lucky to break Lowestoft pots, eh, Puck? Suppose——" Sally's face grew thoughtful.

She left the pony's side and retraced her steps to the house.

Lunch-time. Rymer himself was ringing the gong as she entered the hall. His back looked martyred, as Sally noticed. There was an atmosphere of martyrdom everywhere, she decided; and Granny gave a little sigh as she passed the spot on the stairs where the Lowestoft jar had stood for so long. Sally, feeling righteously sympathetic, took her grandmother's arm as they went into the dining-room together, and gave it a little squeeze.

"And now, to go on with what you were saying," said Sally invitingly in her most pleasant voice.

"To go on with——" Granny looked flustered. She was helping herself to vegetables. "To go on with, my dear child. *What* do you mean? I haven't seen you to speak to for the last half-hour——"

"What you said *last*," remarked Sally,

pleasantly conversational. "Now *don't* get worried, darling. ' I've too many spare hours on my hands,' you said. *So I have!* Well, that brings us to what I'm *always* asking. You've come round to my point of view, Granny darling, utterly and entirely. I've been asking for months and months and months——" Sally's voice rose.

"Potatoes, Miss Sally?" Rymer's voice at her elbow sounded severe, and almost menacing in its displeasure.

But no potato should stem Sally's flood of eloquence now it had reached its flood. "No, thank you," she motioned him away.

"*So*, Granny, you and I are really *agreed* now, are we not? I've too many hours on my hands. Those were your words. So——"

"My dear Sally!" Granny had been upset before. Now she laid down her fork. "You must excuse me, my darling. Old heads can't stand quite as much as young ones. I'm just a little worried." She left the room.

"Poor Granny." Sally rose too. "I'll come——"

To her horror and fury she found herself intercepted at the door, and by none other than old Rymer! Between her and the door he stood.

" Miss Sally, you'll excuse me, miss. It's beyond my place, perhaps, miss ; but it's more than blood can stand. Hafter hall these years to 'ave the old mistress worrited to death. Your ways is past finding out, miss ; that is what it comes to. Harle-bargle—yes, I've said it. And if the Captain himself was here I'd stand up and confess. It may be *Hinjun* ways, miss ; but seems to me— And now the Hold Lowestoft what she's prized so long, and then——"

" Rymer, will you kindly—" Sally drew herself up.

" You'll excuse me, Miss Sally, but——"

For answer Sally turned her back. It was perfectly easy, and quite fairly dignified to disappear through the window. How Rymer *dared!* Her face was crimson with passion, but she'd taken in the gist of his remarks all the same, for Sally was no fool. But she was going straight to her grandmother, of course, just as she'd intended to before Rymer interfered. Rymer was spoilt, that was it ! And how he *dared* to mention Dad, as though Dad would *agree* with what he'd said. Sally tried to hum, but she found herself wondering for all that whether perhaps Dad *would* have agreed. She was rather glad when the postman held her up, perforce, for a moment on the drive.

(2,432)

" Would you wish to take the post, miss ? The Indian mail, Miss Sally."

" Thanks." Sally still held her head high.

It was holding a letter, then, that she arrived almost at once in Granny's morning-room. Mrs. Heath was sitting there ; there was a scent of eau de Cologne in the room, and her handkerchief was pressed to her forehead.

" Darling," she began apologetically.

" Darling," began Sally almost apologetically too. Then, as her grandmother opened the foreign envelope, the white head and the golden one bent together over its closely written pages.

" I'm not sure, Sally darling," began her grandmother, a little anxiously, " whether the letter——"

But Sally evidently didn't hear.

" ' The Headmistress of the Beech Trees School writes—' " Almost the first of Dad's sentences opened that way. As, gasping, she finished reading the sentence, Sally gave a squeak.

" *Granny !* I'm to *go ? Granny !* That's what I've said all along I ought to do, *Granny !* Oh, *hurrah !* " Sally rose up and pirouetted round the room. " *Oh !* I shall expire of joy if I can't tell somebody. *Oh !* " Out of the

morning - room and stablewards she raced
until the pony's stall was reached. " Puck ! "
whispered Sally deliriously. " Oh, *Puck!*
It *is* lucky to break Lowestoft vases ; oh,
it *is !* "

CHAPTER II

SALLY MEETS THE BOYS

" WELL, as I was saying, old chap—"
It was none so dusty to be going
back to Beeches again—at least so thought
Pollitt, if only for the rather decent journey
up with old Perry. " As I was saying, we could
rig one up easy——"

" A jolly good notion. *But*, you rattling
ass——"

" Look here, though, we *could*. We'd pick
up some old sheet-iron; that's all we'd need
to make the diaphragms. Twig? Then, if
we connected two bits of it by metal wire,
and stretched it jolly tight, there we'd *be*. A
telephone between the rooms. And if we
get those next-door studies this half, you
know——"

" Well," his chum was listening intently;
" and even if *not*."

" Good for you. Pass it outside the windows,
you mean? Well, why not? The idea sprung

on me because one of my cousins was making a swanking row about some notion of his at the engine-works where he's landed. Miles apart the men are apparently, but they rigged up a contraption like that and it worked fine, he said."

" So long, of course, as there's no inter-rupting——"

" O-o-o-oh ! How *bored* I am ! "

Both boys sat up with a jerk. For there was no doubt but that their ears had not deceived them. There *had* been a voice from the farthest corner of the railway carriage in which they sat, and in which also sat—until now dis-regarded as a nonentity—a girl. She was alone, otherwise she might, of course, have been expected to talk. Under the circumstances, however, she had *not* been expected to speak. The strength of her utterance surprised them. They were surprised still further in another instant. Evidently she was no harmless lunatic at large with a mania for monologue, as they'd begun to imagine ; she was addressing *them*.

" Well, and wouldn't *you* be bored to bits if you were me ? Telephones, telegraphs, telescopes, and tell-tale-tits—all those things bore me to *tears*. You can't imagine how machinery of all sorts makes me shudder ! And I've been sitting in this corner listening to you, feeling more and more and more depressed. If you'd only talk of something more interesting."

A dead silence fell upon the boys. Where did this unwelcome and unsophisticated maiden spring from ?

" About *animals*, for instance," suggested Sally in her brightest tone. " Anything alive is, to *me* anyway, *far* more interesting than machinery. *Any* kind of machine — from bathing-machines to machine-guns—should be, in my opinion, forbidden as conversation by *law*. If you'll talk about animals, I'll listen and love to. (And travelling *is* so tiring, isn't it ?) I'd even join in." Then as the silence, relieved only by shufflings of feet on the part of her travelling companions, seemed unlikely to be broken by any masculine tone of voice, Sally tried again. " Or even *schools*. I'd love to hear what your school is like, you know. I'm going to school myself ; and you're going back, aren't you, too ? "

Thus addressed, both Perry and Pollitt lamely tried to do the polite.

" Yes—er—what I mean to say is, yes, *rather*. We're going back." They were beginning to hate this girl. What on earth did she get into their carriage for, for one thing ? And why on earth, when she *was* in it, couldn't she sit still and keep her mouth shut ? They fell into grim silence again.

" Oh, well, if you won't talk, you won't," remarked Sally lightly. " I must say it wasn't like this on board ship. You'd have been *taboo* by this time. It's really only the merest good *manners*—" She spoke scathingly.

" She's evidently only just landed or something. Tell her about the pigeons, old chap," suggested Pollitt in a rather hoarse and desperate whisper.

" Er — fond of *birds ?* " remarked Perry desperately. " *Birds*, you know, little chaps with wings." He feebly imitated the motion of flying in his certainty that this individual must have arrived recently from outlandish parts.

" Rather ! I love them." Sally had taken up a magazine, but now she threw it down with relish. " I adore them. In India, you know, there aren't any of those ripping little robins and thrushes and things that my grandmother's got building in her garden. I say, tell me, have you got any ? "

" Carriers. Pigeons, you know." But once warmed up on this subject, which was dear to the hearts of both of them, the boys found little difficulty in keeping the conversation ball rolling. It was plain, also, that Sally was not an *ordinary* girl, so they had both mentally agreed. She certainly seemed to have little knowledge of this particular country and its ways anyhow. India, she'd said. Well, perhaps that explained her airy-fairy manners. "Carriers. Well, we're training them, you know. In term-time——"

"You mean at your *school*? Oh, I say, what *ripping* things they must do at boy-schools." Sally sighed enviously.

"Well, things aren't so dusty at girl-schools either, come to that. I've got a cousin—" Perry was growing talkative. "They let you have hobbies and things. The pigeons, well, they're *that*—a hobby, I mean. Pollitt, here, and I—well, we swapped two rather rotten stamp collections for a half-dozen carriers last term. We're going to train 'em to long-carrying practice, we rather think, when we get back."

"I say, do explain."

The boys were only too pleased to do so. They proceeded.

Anything was better than the terrible tension which had pervaded the carriage before. Besides, this girl wasn't so bad after all, perhaps, they'd decided. She was keen enough on the pigeons anyway. The next half-hour passed interestingly enough for the whole company concerned.

" Provided we're not absolutely bowed *down* with impots, you know." Perry was winding his tale to a close. The circumstances of the pigeon swap had been explained ; the advantages of a systematic pigeon-post to chaps at school ; the difficulties which the pair had had to overcome before the housekeeper would allow the birds to remain for the hols. in charge of the boot-boy. " And so, provided we're not absolutely bowed *down* with impots, we mean to train 'em this term. There's rather a no-end decent little tea-gardens place on the hills. ' Smugglers' Tea Cosy ' it's called ; run by a rather decent old servant, you know, who used to be at our school but bunked from there when she married, and runs the tea-gardens place now. Well, we have tea there fairly often, and we rather think of walking the little chaps out there and letting 'em find their way back. For practice, you see. And in time, if we start training 'em that way, we'd rig up a fairly systematic post——"

" I say ! And send letters ? I never heard of such a thing ! Dad told me that some of the rajahs keep pigeons, but just for pleasure, you know. Great houses they have built for them, and spend heaps of money."

Sally was growing more and more interested.

And the boys were growing more tolerant of Sally.

" Do they, eh ? Well, it's a frightful pity it's not carriers that they keep instead of those fancy breeds. Carriers are the ticket ; there's some use in 'em. What, letters, why, rather ! They were used, homers were—in the war and before that—for carrying messages. Siege of Paris even. Why, a pigeon that's jolly well trained can carry messages a hundred miles or more. They've even used them for carrying Stock Exchange messages between London and Paris, and beat the mail, and chaps made fortunes by it. Twig ? " But as the pigeon-owners waxed eloquent Sally grew weary again.

" I say, you *won't* grow too educational again, will you ? " she entreated them sweetly. But even before she had completed her sentence the pair had sprung to their feet and were beginning to haul bags down from the rack.

" Er—sorry. Well, we're off now, though. This next station's ours. *You're* going to school, aren't you, didn't you say ? Can we be of any use ? Hope it's a decent school. You're new, of course."

They were both astounded by the look of dignity which sprang into Sally's eye.

" *New !* I certainly did not tell you that

I was ' new,' as you call it. *New!* And my school is topping, thanks."

" Fairly put our feet into it—deep," remarked Pollitt to Perry in an undertone, as they strapped up a case. " Yet I thought——"

" You may very kindly lift down my suit-case from the rack if you will," said Sally in a forgiving tone.

Both boys sprang awkwardly to obey. Then the train drew up with a jerk. " I say—er—this is the junction. Don't know if you're changing ? "

" Thank you. I do *hope* that boot-boy's looked properly after your pigeons. Good-bye." Sally bowed to them in an auntly way.

" Not such a rotten sort of girl after all, was she ? " remarked Pollitt, " when you come to know her a bit."

" Quite all right," agreed his chum, stepping out. " Seemed keen on those pigeons, which showed jolly good sense anyway. Wonder what school she's for ; somewhere up the line, I suppose. Beech Trees, perhaps, where my cousin is ; she'd have to change on to the loop-line for that and get out next station. Said she'd been there some time, didn't she ? Or *did* she ? Fact was I got the idea she'd just landed from Timbuctoo or some such spot when she first spoke. Bit of a mystery some-how."

" Here, I say, talking of mysteries, glad you reminded me. I picked up the rippingest book in the hols. *Mystery of the Yellow Room* it called itself. I advise you——"

The walk wore on. For they were walking up to school; they generally did. It was far more pleasant, after being cooped up in the train, to stretch one's legs and stride out instead of rattling up in one of the musty flies. The Beeches lay two and a half miles outside the sleepy county town, and once clear of the street of shops the hills were all around at once.

" The other chaps will have mostly arrived by this time," remarked Perry.

Pollitt agreed. It was likely. The other chaps were all of them from longer distances, and they caught the express from town. Pollitt and Perry, by reason of their respective homes being in the fairly near neighbourhood, generally tootled up late in the afternoon in a slow market train, and arrived at The Beeches some time before supper and first roll-call. It was fairly dusky, then, when after their walk they turned in at the gates leading to the well-known drive.

" Here we are, and here we are, and here we are *again!* " remarked Pollitt with some relief, shifting a rather heavy bag from one arm to the other. " And in two ticks, my lad, I'll be——"

But his remark was destined never to be finished, for suddenly out of the gathering gloom there issued an unexpected apparition.

" Well," exclaimed a voice which tried hard to be cocksure but which very nearly failed, " I *am* glad to see you. Fact is, I rather hoped, when I found out——"

Sally of the train emerged, head held high; but as she enunciated her welcoming remarks her voice gave a sudden little choke.

CHAPTER III

ENTER JOSY

" YOU'LL be late, Josy."

" Oh, bother ! *bother !* BOTHER ! And I can't find that slipper. Did I pack it, or didn't I ? Are any of you wearing it as well as your own ? Did anybody *ever* come down to tea on first night without shoes, do you think ? You're not *going*, you wretches, are you ? *Oh*, don't eat my scrambled eggs ! "

But they *were* going. They were gone, leaving the dormitory pickle behind. The tea-bell on first night meant much : scrambled eggs for famished maidens who had dined insufficiently in the train on sandwiches and chocolates ; a meeting with old friends *en masse* for the first time in the term ; the first chance of surveying the features of freshers who would never be so new again after to-night, and of deciding whether or not they were worthy of a place at Beech Trees. Down to tea flocked the girls at the first summons of the bell. There were no rules on first night, but off they flew.

Josy sat on her heels on the floor considering. "Under the beds I've looked. Some of them may have tidied it into their cubies by mistake, though they say they haven't. You bet they'll eat my scrambled eggs. Or else they'll be cold. I wish—" She sighed and gave a leap into the air. "My suit-case!"

It was there. Packed at the last moment. "I remember. Mummy said that loose bow was a disgrace, and sewed it on herself." Josy slipped it on and followed the rest downstairs equably enough. She would be last in, of course. Five minutes ago she had heard the chairs being dragged in over the wooden floor of the dining-hall. That meant that Matron had said grace and that the meal was in full swing. "Well, anyhow, it's first night." Josy proceeded in leisurely fashion along the passage.

"Thank you. I—er—*drove* up." A high clear voice sounded up the stairs from the front hall as she came down.

Was this a new girl? Josy slowed her steps. Even if she were to lose her scrambled eggs she *must* see what this new girl was like. It *might* even be a new mistress, she decided, for the voice didn't sound at all freshery or shy. Even Josy, who was not known for shyness, remembered that a year ago she couldn't possibly have dared to reply to Miss Shirley's greetings in that tone.

" You *drove* up ? You are Sara Heath, are you not ? We were growing anxious about you. Your grandmother has just wired, and Miss Dean was just about to reply that you had not arrived."

" Really ! " The tone was a little *more* freshery now, Josy decided. She couldn't help hearing, for the voices were sounding right through the empty corridors. " Well, you can reply, can't you, that I'm here and *perfectly* safe. Poor Granny, she *does* worry so." The newcomer's tone took on a pitying note. " Yes, I drove up. From a—that junction place——"

" You mean from Lewes ? Why, you should have changed there into a loop-line train. *Such* a long drive you must have had."

" But a long drive *is* so nice and refreshing in the evening, isn't it ? "

Josy could almost *hear* Miss Shirley's breath being taken away. Her own came in a gasp. For a new girl to speak like *that*. Quite unconsciously she stood stock still in the middle of the hall and stared at a girl rather taller than herself ; almost fourteen years old, Josy decided. Thin and erect and sparkle-eyed. There was, however, a " something " in the expression of the eyes which made Josy gaze. She realized, whether Miss Shirley did or not, that the last words had not been meant at all impertinently.

For once, when Josy had been small, she had been taken out hunting by Dad. " In at the death " Dad had wangled her somehow. Strange ! For an instant, *now*, she had been reminded of the look in the eyes of the fox *then*. It had been cornered, and the hounds— Josy would never let herself remember that part. Every one had applauded her riding, and the M.F.H. had handed her the brush. But instead of being proud she had wept all the way home. Dad had been ashamed of her, so he'd said, till she'd told him, seated hard on her saddle and trying to control her tears. But then " Well, well, well ! " Dad had said ; " Mummy was right, perhaps, and it's a bit young to bring you." And Josy hadn't hunted again for two years. Funny, wasn't it, she told herself, that she should remember that look in the fox's eyes at the sight of this rather strange new girl. She turned rather quickly in the direction of the dining-hall.

" Josy, Josy," called Miss Shirley, becoming aware of her presence. Josy turned again. " The others are at tea Josy," said Miss Shirley. " You are late. And Sara Heath has just arrived. She is to sleep in your dormitory, so take her with you upstairs to wash her hands. She is very tired and dusty after an unnecessarily long drive." There was a rather severe note in Miss Shirley's usually cheery tone. " I will explain to Matron that you will come down soon."

Matron was taking tea-duty. That meant that the eggs would be sent back to the kitchen to be kept warm. Josy led the way upstairs.

" Well, I've got here at last," said the stranger, sitting on the edge of the first bed with rather a breathless bang.

Josy felt breathless too. She was beginning to wonder if her imagining in the corridor had been just a mistake. *Could* it have been ? She stared soberly at the stranger.

" Well ! " The newcomer looked back at her. If she *had* needed pulling together, there evidently was now no further need. " *Well !* "

" We're not really supposed to sit on the counterpanes," put in Josy, feeling most uncommonly shy before this unfreshery fresher. " Or we get into the most awful rows."

" Good ! I like rows. They clear the air," replied the newcomer, sitting hard. " That's partly the fun of school I should rather think. Who makes them—the rows, I mean ? Any more things that I'm not supposed to do, eh ?

Out with them, and then I'll decide whether I'll do them or not. I'm Sally Heath, by the way ; and though I've already been introduced to you as Sara, I've never heard the name since the day I was christened ; and then I yelled so loudly at the sound of it that they would have unchristened me if it hadn't happened to be too late. Hideous name, Sara, don't you think ? "

" I like Sally best," said Josy, dimpling.

" And I like—you," Sally suddenly smiled back. " Josy your name is, I know, because I heard that teachery person in the high collar call you that. It suits you, I think. Josy, can you keep a secret ? "

" Oh yes," said Josy at once. She knew that she could.

" Good for you. Well, then, I'm thinking of telling you one. You can believe it or not as you like, but I decided to, in the cab before I'd ever seen you. ' If the first girl I meet is a futile-looking creature with a pigtail I *won't* tell her,' I thought ; ' but if she looks sporty and has bobbed hair, then I *may*.' Well, there you *are*."

Josy felt quite taken aback by this remark. " I'm sure," began she, feeling very much honoured, " that we ought to go down to tea."

Never before had she been commissioned to

take a fresher upstairs on arrival. Generally the honour fell to older girls. Josy was only twelve, and nearly the youngest in the dorm. *This* girl, so she decided, would be second eldest. For Sheila was the dorm. head this term now that Doris had left. Last term Doris had ruled the roost very despotically indeed, and Josy had been in great and awful dread. But *this* term, with Sheila, who was " as weak as wax," to quote the general opinion in the dorm., and this new Sally as the oldest members, Josy already saw rather jolly times ahead.

Dormitory feasts ! Could it possibly be that their room also would share in the delights which other dormitories boasted. These things were winked at at Beech Trees by some of the heads, but Doris had remained adamantine to her last day in spite of entreaties from her dorm. Josy woke from a dream of hitherto unimagined bliss to her protégée's next remark.

" Well, any more ' oughts ' ? Do you do exactly as you're told at Beech Trees ? Or do some of you act, just occasionally, on your own ? "

" Well, Dorm. Two had a serial ghost story that lasted every night last term. The girls told it in turns." Josy supplied the information breathlessly.

" Good for them. Did you go along and listen to it ? Dorm. Two's next door, isn't it ? I saw the number painted up."

" Go *along* and *listen ! Why*, as though—" Shades of Doris and departing discipline.

" Why *not*, if it was worth listening to ; but hardly any ghost tales *are*."

Sally was in her most bragging and anxious-to-impress mood. She stared down at the smaller girl with sparkling eyes. " Dorm. Two shan't have things all to itself *this* term," bragged Sally.

It was at that instant that along the corridor came Sybil, prefect of the landing—stumpy, sturdy, stentorian of voice, but sterling at heart.

" Josy, you there ? "

" Yes, Sybil." Josy sprang to attention.

" I hear you're looking after a new girl." Sybil entered. " How d'you do ? Hope you'll like Beech Trees. Washed and all that, eh ? Well, then, Josy will take you down. Don't dawdle, please. You're late for tea as it is, and——"

" I *am* rather hungry, and so I am just going down. You needn't have troubled," Sally broke in upon the speech in icily gracious tones.

" And so," continued the prefect, as though she had not noticed the interruption, " you'd better both make haste." She disappeared through the door as she spoke.

" And who may the lordling be ? " inquired Sally aloud. " A rajah-ess in mufti ? "

" S-sh ! Oh, s-s-sh ! " whispered Josy un-easily. " It's a prefect. She's head girl of this landing, you know."

" *Head !* Who's she *head* of ? " inquired Sally briskly. " Anyway, she won't be head girl over *me*."

CHAPTER IV

SALLY HOLDS THE STAGE

" OO-O-OH ! Sal-*lee !* "
"It's absolutely true, I'm sure. The natives are absolutely uncanny. As for magicking snakes, *that's* simply nothing ; I've *seen* them at it scores of times. But listen ! Well, they'll throw a rope up into the air as far as you can see, you know, and they'll utter a charmy sort of speech, and there it *hangs !* Sort of suspended in the air. And then up runs a little grinning native boy. (Yes, while the rope's hanging suspended from nothing !) And when he reaches the tip-top *tip*, there he stands grinning. And then—well, after him climbs up the native magician, and cuts him up into *scraps* with a native sort of spear. Brings down the pieces, too (yes, he does), in a basket ! Shows them all round." Sally spoke with a relish as she embroidered her theme more and more. "And then——"

"O-o-o-oh ! Sal-*lee !* " The juniors of the dorm. sat up in bed and longed for night-lights.

It was quite a relief when Sheila's common or garden voice boomed out again, " Look here, Sally, stow it, and let's get to sleep ! "

For it wasn't the first tir e that Sheila had interrupted, nor the second, nor the third. Yet still the tales poured equably forth from the new girl's lips.

" Weak as wax," Sheila might be ; but things were getting beyond a joke, as even one of her easy-going temperament realized.   This was the third night since the newcomer's appearance ; and on each of the first two several hours had been docked from the dormitory's rest.   Head dorm. girls were supposed to manage the occupants of their rooms themselves, as Sheila knew ; but—   This new Sally was a very great " but " indeed.   She seemed to have gained an ascendancy over the dormitory in an altogether unprecedented way.

" Look *here*," burst in Sheila in desperation. After all she *was* a Fifth girl, and Sally, though she rivalled the dorm.'s head in inches, was far below in learning, having been relegated after the entrance exam.-papers to rather a mean position in the Fourths.   " Look *here !* Shut *up !* And if that's the Indian rope trick that you think you're describing, it's a fake.   All the papers say so.   There's never been a person who saw it.   *All* those Indian tricks are fakes."

" Fakes ! They're *not !* " If Sheila had
wished to bring peace and slumber to her dorm.
she had set about the business in quite the
wrong way. " *Fakes !* "

" Well, none of the kids will sleep, anyway,
for funk," grumbled Sheila wearily, longing for
slumber herself after a strenuous day.

" *Funk ! Rot !* We love it ! " chorused
Hesther and Dorothy, as though last term's
dorm. discipline was as forgotten as the last
year's snows !

For nobody cares to be labelled as funks,
however funky they may be. Sheila's efforts
on behalf of the juniors were strangled at
birth. She was conscious, too, horribly, that
last term none of the " kids " would have *dared*
to raise their voices in that almost impertinent
manner. Even Josy, who might be a pickle
but who certainly had been a very different
kind of pickle last term from the kind that
Sally promised to be, seemed somehow hand
in glove with the newcomer.

" I'll tell you *what !* " burst out Sally
firmly. " I'll *prove* it. I'll *do* the mango
trick in the dorm. one night. *I* understand
magic, though you mayn't believe it. *Fakes*,
indeed ! You *wait*." Her voice lowered itself
mysteriously. " Ever heard of *hyp*notism ? "
said Sally.

" O-o-o-oh ! Sal-*lee !* " came the intoxicating refrain.

" Well, anyhow," Sheila began once more in the infinitely weary tone of one groping helplessly towards slumber. " Well, anyhow——"

" *Will you kindly explain* the meaning of this outrageous noise at this time of night ? " The question hurtled suddenly through the dorm. door in stentorian tones.

A dead silence fell. Only for a second, however. The juniors might be conscious of a desperate longing to disappear to the bottom of their respective beds for ever ; Sheila might be conscious of a feeling almost of relief at the appearance of this deliverer, however disciplinary might be her methods ; but Sally was only conscious of a desire to exchange as quickly as possible some return service in repartee. This was Sybil, of course—the head of the corridor. How *dared* she ?

" You've only to stand there *listening outside the door* a little longer, and then you'll not need to ask for an explanation," retorted Sally briskly.

" Sheila, I am speaking to *you*. You're head here. Have you not control over your dorm. ? " Sybil's voice crashed in before the end of Sally's remark, but she must have heard part of it anyway.

" Yes, Sybil. Awfully sorry, Sybil." Sheila rose on an elbow which felt nerveless from need of sleep.

" *Can* you manage your dorm. yourself ? " Sybil's tone sounded sinister. " For you've only to report them (or any *one* of them) to *me*, you know, if you can't. And *I'll* take the matter up." Sybil was on the war-path ; there was no doubt of that.

" Yes, Sybil. Awfully sorry, Sybil. They'll be all right now, Sybil." Sheila spoke apologetically, and sounded direly remorseful. She was too good-hearted and well-meaning to report any of them, even Sally, to whose influence this midnight visitation was certainly due.

" Then, if you *can* manage them, will you do so, please. I give you three minutes to settle down in here." Sybil turned.

" *Manage* us ! " Sally broke in quickly. " *Manage* us ! I'd like to see anybody manage *me* ! The ' outrageous noise,' as you call it, Sybil, was merely a discussion on Indian magic led by myself."

" *Then* "—the head of the corridor turned crisply—" you will kindly report yourself to me to-morrow evening, Sara Heath. After supper, before bedtime, you understand." Sybil was gone.

" Right," called Sally into the darkness.

" O-o-o-oh, Sal-*lee !* " came a hissing but wholly terrified whisper from the junior beds.

" Well, you're in for it now." Sheila turned over. " And you deserve it. I wouldn't have reported you, but—" She yawned.

And even Sally realized that there would be no further conversation in the dorm. that night. The juniors were too subdued ; the head was too sleepy ; and she, herself—now she came to realize it—was not so much inclined to talk as she had been. To-morrow night. *Pooh !* She could make that Sybil sit up. Airs and graces ! Prying and peering round. Sally, too, turned over on her side and fell asleep instantly.

To experience a medley of exciting and entrancing dreams, in each of which she herself figured as the chief, but in each of which, strange to say, Josy figured too—Josy who had been Sally's first acquaintance at Beech Trees. In all Sally's dream-escapades Josy followed her, watching with her wide-open frank blue eyes. For, so far, Josy remained the only girl at Beech Trees whom Sally thought she would ever care two straws for as a friend. There had been something in Josy's attitude on the day of the new girl's arrival which, to Sally, had been like water to a fainting man. She had felt, somehow, that here was a girl—even though she might be fully two years younger than Sally herself—who would be worth making friends with ; who could be trusted with a confidence. Josy couldn't be more than thirteen, but she possessed more " reserve " than did Sheila, the dormitory head. Yes, Josy was to be Sally's ally ; Sally had decided that ; and half of her braggadocio in the dorm. was calculated to impress Josy rather than the rest.

Where the others exclaimed, Josy listened silently. Sally wanted to impress Josy most of all. For she had quite taken in the fact that her chief friend at Beech Trees must, perforce, be a girl younger than herself. She had realized already that her own contemporaries in years had absorbing interests of their own, and that they were not in the least anxious nor likely to admire *her*. Also, Sally found herself in class far removed from girls of her own age. They were all placed much higher in the school. Well, she meant to be a leader, and she didn't much care whom she led. But she wanted Josy for her friend and admirer—that she *did* want. Josy, of the very frank, the very wide and very blue-eyed gaze, was to be Sally's friend.

She would have been surprised if she had known that Josy, too, was dreaming, and of Sally herself, that night. Dreaming a dream of how Sally and she were hunting—riding,

riding, riding over the Down. And of how suddenly, while she was admiring Sally, thinking how wonderful she was, everything had changed. And she had been alone—not even with Daddy—in at the death, like that dreadful day. And the fox ! And Sally again !

Josy had sat up in bed uttering a mournful sobbing cry. " *Oh ! oh ! oh !* "

" I say, cheer up. Dreaming of mango tricks, eh ? " It was Sally's voice through the cubie. " Woa there ! Steady. Woa ! "

" *Oh !* " Josy was awake now, and horribly ashamed of herself, and trembling too. She had had this dream—part of it, anyway—before, and it always left her gaspy. " *Oh !* " She tried to keep the choke out of her voice. " It's only—— "

" Steady. Catch on." Sally thrust a fist through the curtain. She herself had been wakened from a stream of dreams, and, only half-awake, she seemed quite a different Sally. Josy, perhaps for the first time, realized that Sally was lovable as well as wonderful. In two minutes she was asleep again, with her own brown paw held tight in Sally's brown one.

Sally didn't go to sleep for quite a long time after that. She felt as she lay there grasping the little paw as she'd felt sometimes towards Puck the pony. When she did sleep her dreams were filled with her own escapades, of course; but Josy figured in all of them again. And all the time, till morning, Sally was conscious that she still grasped protectingly Josy's small and muscular fist.

CHAPTER V

A COCOA-PARTY WITH A CURTAIN

"COME in, please. Yes, I was waiting."
Sybil rose up from a basket-chair.

The prefects' rooms at Beech Trees were
very comfortable domains. Miss Dean had
seen to that. Where other girls of less importance in the school slept in curtained cubies,
with a severely monastic space allotted to them
for necessaries, the Sixth Form corridor-heads
possessed four walls of solid plaster, a window,
and a door apiece. More than that, each of
the heads' rooms was furnished as a study-
bedroom. A small writing-table, which could
be used likewise as a tea-table, was there ; a
basket-chair, and a Liberty curtain, which hid all
traces of ablutionary implements. It was little
wonder that to own one of these abodes some
day was the aim and gaping hope of the very
smallest Beech-Trees-ites, and that the owners
themselves, already august as being prefects
and Sixth Formers, attained an almost Olympian

position in the eyes of the school when one of these rooms became their own. For there were twelve Sixth Form girls at Beech Trees and only six corridors. The possession of these rooms was arranged by a general mistress's vote. Sybil Hartling had been elected two terms ago to the coveted position : she meant to do her best by her corridor, too, and so far she had succeeded as well as she had hoped. Corridor A had been a credit to Beech Trees, a model territory.

But the scene in Dormitory Three of the night before had been an awakening. Such a happening had been unprecedented during her reign. Sybil, wise with the result of nearly two years' prefecting, had thought the matter over. This new girl had got to be tackled right off, that was certain. Lecture her ? That had jolly well got to come, of course, but not bang off. After much more cogitation, then, than Sally guessed at, Sybil made up her mind.

" Come in," said the corridor head equably enough as Sally entered.

Sally was looking as equable as sounded Sybil's tone ; as cool as a cucumber. Owing to the constant reiteration of Dorothy's and Hesther's hopes that she " wouldn't have too bad a time," owing to the rather anxious look in Josy's blue eyes, Sally felt like an excited war-horse pawing the ground and scenting battle. Her eyes were dancing as she entered. Her voice sounded like that of a conventional lady-caller rather than a refractory damsel " up for a row." " Tha-ank you. Come in, shall I ? Tha-anks." She knew that the others were listening in the corridor on their way bedwards. Anyhow Dorothy and Hesther. She felt a little more flat when the door closed behind her. " Wh-at a dear little room you have," said Sally briskly.

Sybil was clever. She grasped at this opening. She came forward. " Yes, sit down, please. Sit here, where you can see it." Sally found herself in the basket-chair. " We corridor heads always invite new girls on our landing into our room first week."

" For rows ? " There was the glint of battle in Sally's eye.

" No, not for rows." Sybil evidently didn't notice the glint. Her back was turned, and she was already bending over a gas-ring on which a kettle hissed. " For this. Will you have some cocoa ? " She was pouring it out. " We don't believe in ' rows,' as you call them, at Beech Trees. That word's down and under ; relegated to the story-book sort of girls. Do you take sugar ? "

" Oh ! " Sally was feeling more than a

trifle nonplussed. It was all very well to lead the juniors, but she didn't seem so sure-footed here somehow. " Sugar ; thank you. Oh, but *I* think ' rows ' rather fun." She spoke slowly.

Sybil was ready for her. " Yes. Well, perhaps you *would*, you know. Just home from India, aren't you ? I suppose you can't *help* being so awfully ignorant about schools." Sybil's tone was almost pitying. She looked Sally down from top to toe. " It's hard on you, but you'll learn. Have a biscuit ? They're very nice ones."

Sally had a feeling that things weren't going right, for her. She was already drinking Sybil's cocoa. Oh, why hadn't she refused it ? Well, anyhow, it was ripping, and she might as well finish it ; and the biscuits were macaroons ! She meant to hold her own for all that.

" Hard on me ? " panted Sally. " But—" What should she say with these grave prefecty eyes looking into hers so horribly compassion- ately. She felt almost drowning in a sea of common sense. " Ignorant of school ways," of course she was ! Nobody knew that fact better than Sally herself. It was *because* she felt that the others might have noticed it that she had been forced to brag so much to keep her end up. On that first day when she'd arrived, after—(Oh, she thrust back the remembrance of the secret episode far from her; nobody should know). She smiled. " Ignorant was the word you used, wasn't it ? " said Sally in her most conventional grown-up voice. " Well, I wonder how India would suit *you*? Have you ever been there ? "

" No." Sybil bit into a macaroon.

Sally took heart. " Oh ! then it's ' hard lines ' for *you*, isn't it ? But perhaps one day you'll get the chance." She was going full tilt now. " We have so *many* things to do out there, you know, that coming to school seems such a *very* little thing after——"

Sally took a gulp of cocoa. What should she say next ? Tales of big-game shooting and pig-sticking, of native magic and snake bites raced into her brain. Should she bring them all in, or——

" Well "—it was Sybil's grave, even voice— " for my own part I would rather be at school now, and go abroad later. From results that I've seen in awfully spoilt kiddies brought up by ayahs, you know, I'd rather——"

Did Sybil mean anything personal ? Sally looked up suddenly. It was *as* she looked up that the awful and unbelievable thing happened ! Her eyes fell upon a photograph, pinned on to the calendar by the fireplace, not a yard away. A photograph of her hostess,

Sybil—common sense and golf-clubs complete
—*and* by her side the form of somebody else
whose image called up Sally's direst funk.
Everything was forgotten but *this*. She sat,
holding the empty cocoa cup, staring, thought
Sybil, blankly into space.

" Poor kid. I had to give her that last,"
thought the well-meaning prefect. " She's not
a bad fresher. She will probably find her own
level without any more aid from me." She
rose. " Like to have a look round my room
before you go back ? " said she.

Sally grasped at the idea. She took an
urgent step forward in the direction of the
portrait. It was true. There was no mistak-
ing the likeness. It was true.

" Yes ; you've spotted me." Sybil was
smiling with prefecty benignity. " Taken last
hols. Staying with my cousin, I was. We're
the greatest pals, he and I. See lots of each
other in the holidays. We're both jolly keen
on golf, and mean to write a book together,
like the Wethereds did, later on. His school—"
She said more.

Sally heard every word that she said. Every
word made her feel worse. Oh, to get out of
this room quickly before committing herself
further. " Thank you very much." Almost
it did not sound like Sally's voice at all. " For

—er—the cocoa, you know. I'm rather tired."
She essayed a yawn. She backed to the door.

"Right." Sybil held out a golfy fist with
a punch to it, and shook her hand warmly.
"Don't forget, eh? Rows are kids' things,
and old-fashioned at that. We don't have 'em
here. And you're bound to be tired, you
know, as you say, after last night. Probably
the rest are too." Sybil grinned again in
prefecty fashion. Then, as the door closed
on the retreating fresher, the head of the corridor
sank thankfully into the wide-armed basket-
chair. "Pulled it off, what?" said Sybil to
herself. "Though I own that at first I rather
wondered whether I would. She's a specimen
of ayah-trained childhood, if ever there was
one. Wanting *me* to go to India before I'm
through the matric.!"

Sybil hastily swallowed the remains of the
cocoa, put the macaroons in a tin box and, forgetting the existence of Sally, settled down
to her Latin translation in the confident assurance that there would be no more trouble with
Dormitory Three.

As for Sally, two anxious heads peeped from
the two cubies where Dorothy and Hesther
were undressing.

"Sally, I say, did you——"

"Shut up," returned Sally urgently, before

she realized what construction would be put upon the utterance. She had reached her cubie and surveyed her own pink-flushed cheeks and startled eyes—which the others must have noticed too !—and had heard their whispered " *Whew-w-w !* Sybil *does* give it hot ! " before she, like the worm, turned.

But Sheila had already declared, " Shut up, kids, or you'll get it hot too, if you don't wank into bed before Sister comes," thus adding flames to Sally's fire of affliction. She stamped within her cubie in mingled horror and hate.

" Shut up, I say. If you think, if you *dare* to think that I'm a bit bothered because of anything *Sybil* may have said, you're wrong— absolutely wrong. If you think——"

" Lights out, now." Sister entered. " Undress in the dark, Sally. Yes, I know where you've been, and *why*. I gave my permission. But you'll have to undress in the dark all the same." She disappeared.

There was no general talk in the dorm. that night—no tales of magic. Sally, hastening out of her garments, heard Hesther and Dorothy turn over in their respective beds, and knew that they fell asleep at once, both in serene assurance that Sally had knuckled down ! Sheila thought so too. Did Josy ? Josy hadn't even peeped through the cubie ; she hadn't said a word.

Should she tell Josy the great, the horrible secret ? Should she ? She lay and deliberated, with her nails dug into the palms of her hand.

It was some little while after three slumbering girls were to be heard breathing regularly from three different cubies that suddenly Sally noticed a sound at her side, and a hand drew the curtain between her own and Josy's bed.

" Cheerio ! " said Josy's chirpy voice, but in a very anxious tone. " I couldn't possibly go to sleep till I heard—not possibly, you know. It *isn't* Sybil ; it couldn't be, Sally. What is it, eh ? "

CHAPTER VI

PIGEON POST

OF the other members of her dorm. Sally hadn't taken much notice since *the* night. But she had told Josy. She had told Josy everything. There had been such a comradey sound in Josy's chirpy voice at the moment when she had drawn back the cubie curtains and had peered through that Sally suddenly knew she would tell her — that she must; that she couldn't do anything else. She realized, though without realizing that she realized, perhaps, that what she wanted most of all at that moment was not somebody to applaud her deeds of daring, to act the part of gaping chorus to her bragging remarks, but some one, just like Josy, to be comrade and confidante.

" Listen, I say, then. I'm in a most awful hole," said Sally, in a perfectly new voice, which spoke gaspingly through dry lips.

" The rest are asleep," Josy informed her

comfortingly. " I know all their different kinds of snores."

Thus encouraged, Sally's voice rose a little. " Josy, it was the first day I came."

" Yes." Josy nodded to herself in the darkness of the dorm. Then she *had* been right in what she'd thought. There had been something up that day.

" Josy, the others can't know—they mustn't. Honestly, I absolutely won't let them. They'd think me—" Sally's vanity almost choked her. " I—yes, I did a most idiotic thing on the way here, but it's a secret—altogether a secret. I can't think why I'm telling *you !* "

" Honest Injun, I shan't mention it," put in Josy, more out of sympathy for Sally than with very much anxiety to probe into her secrets.

" Well, then, I tell you flat, I didn't know much about schools when I came. I'll confess that to you, Josy, but only you. But I simply couldn't let Granny's maid travel with me. I knew other girls would roar if I did. Right up to the house Granny told her to come, and she'd have done it ! Well, then, I slipped her at the first change. I did absolutely all right without her, though. I *knew* I would." Sally's voice rose for a moment to its usual cocksure pitch. " I got into the right train beautifully while she was reading papers at the bookstall. There were two boys there." Sally stopped with a little gasp.

" Yes ? " said Josy inquiringly.

" And then it all began. They were jolly enough, but how was I to know about that wretched change at Lewes ? It was really Granny's fault, not mine. If she'd only agreed, as I tried to make her, for me to travel alone, why, then, I'd have looked up the trains, of course, and made sure. But as things were it *wasn't* my fault."

" What wasn't ? " inquired Josy patiently.

" Why, the next thing, of course—that I'm just going to tell you. I got out at a station, and I thought it was *the* station, of course, or naturally I wouldn't have got out. But the name of it was nowhere that I could see, and, to tell the truth, I got a bit muddled when those boys got out there just before me. So I began to ask if there was a change before I got to Beech Trees, and, before I knew where I was, a porter had whisked me into a cab, telling me to drive there. ' It's first day of term there ; they's all driven up,' I heard him say to the driver, and then something about me being, perhaps, some-body's sister. I didn't bother about what he meant. And then, well—" Sally's voice stopped.

" But whatever—" Josy was listening hard.

" It was most awful." The speaker's voice broke into gasps. She had forgotten everything but the story she was telling. " I got there, and I'd got a heavy suit-case. I'd forgotten about my luggage, but, fortunately, it seemed to turn up at school next day all right, owing to its labels. And the driver left me on the step, and then drove off, and I was just going to ring, and then, from everywhere, Josy—through the windows, and inside the door that had a glass front to it, and from everywhere—I saw boys, and boys, and *boys !* " Sally broke off. " Oh, it was a nightmare. I couldn't think what had happened—whether I'd got into a dream, or magic, or something. And I looked, and ' THE BEECHES ' was written on the gate, and I knew it was the idiotic porter's fault, or else the cabman's—it certainly wasn't *mine*—and that I'd come to a boy-school by mistake." Sally's voice shook. There was a sob of mingled rage and wounded pride with the last word.

" But, I say, Sally—" Josy stared. " It didn't *matter* so very much. How *could* it ? Other people make mistakes. You'd only got to ring and *tell* them. They'd have—" Josy's voice was urgent. To her common-sense little round head Sally's confession did not seem so terrible at all. She was not prepared for the next thing that happened.

For Sally, having for the first time got rid of her horror, had suddenly, without the least warning, burst into torrents of weeping. Her head was buried in her pillows; her tears were a flood. "*Matter!* Don't you understand? And *mistakes!* Other people can make them if they like! It meant—oh, I *can't* explain—that you'd all be sure to get to *know!* It made me seem such a *foo-o-o-l!*"

Sally's voice died at last to a sobbing whisper.

Josy suddenly did understand then; helped by the look which she remembered seeing in Sally's eyes on the night of her arrival. She had looked "at bay"; she *had* been "at bay" against things, as only Sally could have been. Josy understood this better, somehow, from having watched Sally's demeanour ever since then. It had been calculated to make her companions "sit up and wonder" at her. It had been, in a way, the courage of despair. "Listen here," said small Josy, leaning over. "But they *don't* know. It's only me. And I don't count." She rubbed her round head comfortingly against Sally's own, like ponies do.

" But there's Sybil—that detestable Sybil, whom I loathe." Sally became suddenly vehement again. " Listen, Josy ; you're a brick, and you *do* count. Listen. I thought that nobody need know till to-night, for things *did* work. Just when I was at my wits' end, with my suit-case in the bushes because I just *wouldn't* ring and make them all laugh at me, and after I'd been to the gate scores of times to see if there was a cab or something that would pass by and take me away—well, *then* something happened that at first seemed the most tremendously good luck." Sally stopped. " Those boys came up," she went on. " The train-boys. The school was theirs. They'd walked from the station. And I told them."

" Well, then ? " said Josy comfortingly.

" Well, that's how I got here. They stopped a milk-cart sort of arrangement thing, and they knew the driver. He was coming this way, and he dropped me here at the gate. He knew the school, this one too, and he belonged to a place where they sell teas or something ; but he didn't get to know any secret about *me* ! I told him Indian stories all the way, and it wasn't so frantically late when I got here, and I'd have given him ten shillings willingly for his trouble, only he wouldn't take it. I carried my suit-case up the drive myself ; I wouldn't let him. Oh, I was so terribly thankful when the maid let me in without seeming to guess anything at all."

" But," began Josy again.

" But now every one *will* know," went on Sally. " You can jolly well bet they will. To-night, Josy, when I was in there with that detestable Sybil, and when I was just about at evens with her, then suddenly— He's her *cousin*," burst out Sally despairingly. " Perry is. The pigeon-boy. I saw her picture ; taken both together they are, in it, and that's *true !* Perry, the one who knew the milk-cart man, the one I talked to most in the train—the nicest one ; and Sybil says that he and she are chums, and tell each other everything, and write pretty nearly every week, and—" Sally began to sob again. " If it wasn't *Sybil*," she said wearily, " perhaps I shouldn't mind so much ; but I simply *couldn't* have her crowing over me, and knowing that I made such a kid's howler and went to the wrong school, and a boy-school instead of a girl-school, and drove up in a milk-cart, and didn't know the right station to go to, and——"

Josy lay still, deliberating. It wasn't easy to comfort Sally. " I say," she suggested suddenly, as being the most obvious and sensible way out of the difficulty to one of her straight and thoroughbred young kind, " you couldn't just go and *tell* Sybil, could you, to-morrow, that you know him? It really was nothing."

" *Tell* her ! I'd rather be drowned in the Ganges," remarked Sally with unction. " No ; but Josy, you've given me an idea. I might tell *him* not to tell her. He was rather a brick, you know."

" But how ? " asked Josy anxiously, fearful lest some fresh escapade of Sally's might bring her into fresh trouble. " We mayn't write letters, except home ones, without permission, you know. Unless they're enclosed home."

" D'you mean to say that Granny—oh, that would be even *worse*." Sally sat up, staring through swollen eyes. " And time's going. *If* that Perry boy writes to Sybil every week like she said, he's pretty certain to write this Sunday. Well, to-morrow's Saturday."

Josy agreed.

" Oh, I say, Josy," begged Sally, " look here. Can't you possibly suggest something ? "

" Except that he mayn't even *think* of mentioning it, I can't, you know. And he mayn't. There's such loads of other things that happen at schools," said Josy, trying tactfully to suggest that Sally's adventure might not figure so largely on Perry's horizon as it did on her own.

But for answer Sally fairly flew. " Mention it ! Of course he will. Josy, I almost wish I hadn't told you, if you're so—" Sally choked.

" Look here, Sally." Josy racked her brains. " I say, I've got an idea. Your saying that to-morrow was Saturday put it into my head. Well, listen. We always go to the ' Smugglers' Tea-Cosy ' on first Saturday afternoon. Made-moiselle takes Lower School walk that day always, while the other mistresses have a time-table meeting with Miss Dean. And Maddy hates anything that isn't plain highroads, so we always go that way. Well, it's just possible that if Perry *was* walking that way with his pigeons, like you said he told you——"

" *Josy !* " Sally threw off all her misery. " He might be. And if I could manage to wangle just to speak to him ! Or else, if I could leave him a note at that ' Tea-Cosy ' place, for when he comes——"

" But there's *rules* about letters, you know, like I said," said Josy, wrinkling up her brows at this fresh suggestion.

" About post-letters ; but I'm not going to post mine. And I must say you needn't make up *new* rules." Sally spoke in an aggrieved way. " Josy, will you walk with me to-morrow, and we'll wangle it through ? "

" Right-o," agreed Josy in rather a bothered tone.

CHAPTER VII

AT THE " SMUGGLERS' TEA-COSY "

SALLY and Josy were walking together. *"En avant, mes enfants !"* Mademoiselle was in a very good mood. On either side of her small Parisienne figure there loomed the lamp-posty and athletic form of a Fourth girl " keen on French." So to-day, although the French mistress loathed *tant de promenades*, and would far rather have been otherwise engaged than in tramping along muddy country roads, yet she philosophically decided that with Gwen and Jean at her side, both feverishly anxious to improve their French accent by spirited conversation, she would, while conducting the Lower School walk, thus kill two birds with one stone. *" Mais oui. A ce* 'Smugglers' Tea-Cosy,' *n'est-ce pas ? Allons. En avant, Beatrice."*

Thus adjured, Beatrice, Fourth-former and leader of the crocodile, set out. On other Saturdays of the term there would certainly be matches, rambles over the Downs, Guide practices, or fixtures of some kind ; but on this particular day the whole English staff at Beech Trees were ensconced in the presence of the headmistress discussing time-tables. The Sixth-formers, and prefects too, were engaged in drawing up lists of possible game fixtures and in marking dorm. lists and Common-room rules. The rest of the school, therefore, secure in the fact that a crocodile walk once a term " couldn't be helped," took to the open road without grumbling. Crocodile walks were not usual at Beech Trees, but no one was grousing. The girls meant to get as much pleasure as possible from the afternoon.

Chums paired off together, keen on holiday experiences, which would be stale after this week. After all, chocs. at the " Smugglers' Tea-Cosy," when they got there, would be ripping, and every one had tons of pocket-money still. And the Downs were looking scrum after the rain, and with the clouds sailing along over the top of them. And any new girls, as the procession wended its way, could be thrilled, as never again, with the tales of the neighbourhood, which boasted ghosts and grues galore.

" See there ? *There's* the church where Povey, the smuggler, is buried, and his tomb's haunted ; it *is !* "

" I say, *those* are the Downs. What ! never heard of them ? Do you take riding, eh ? If you *do*, you'll love cantering over them. We often go. See, we'll have the Downs all round us in a minute. There's a smugglers' track right along from Bradon Harbour, and——"

Thus well-meaning old stagers played cicerone to freshers and extolled the very real beauties of their neighbourhood. Josy, herself conscious of the envious eyes of several of the juniors as she took second place in the ranks by virtue of the height and years of her companion, tried hard to introduce such topics. But Sally was interested in nothing save one all-pervading subject.

" I say, Josy, how soon shall we be there ? "

" At the ' Cosy ' ? Oh, I should say in about three-quarters of an hour. Then Maddy always has a rest, you see, because of her high heels. So we'll have loads of time."

" What about the others ? "

" The others ? Oh, they'll buy chocs., and we might look about. Did you get time to finish the letter ? "

" Rather." Sally's spirits were high. A letter, clearly addressed to Perry at his school, was at present in the pocket of her sports coat. It was brief, but quite sufficiently explicit, she knew, for him to understand its purport.

"Please keep my secret, and don't mention it to any one.—SALLY HEATH," she had written. Both boys had known her name before parting. She didn't want to be more detailed in her letter, but that would do, she decided. "I've got an idea," she remarked. "If we don't see the boys, we could give the letter to that milk-cart man's wife who keeps the tea-place. Then, if the boys come along with the pigeons, she could hand it on."

"We might," said Josy doubtfully. For she knew better than Sally the rabble and rout and ran-tan which usually occurred when twenty-five of the Beech Trees juniors were turned loose like locusts at the "Tea-Cosy." Mary Hinnigan, breathless and excited, had all she could do to deal out her wares and receive payment in the limited space which the cottage-shop provided, without having any free energies with which to attend to private messages, even were they of the S.O.S. variety. "We might run back afterwards, of course," suggested Josy. "Maddy seems most awfully indulgent to-day. She might let us."

As she spoke, the "Smugglers' Tea-Cosy" came into view. It was a little thatched house perched on the side of the Down, just at the roadside, in a position which was nowadays much more public than it had been in the days when the cottage had been used as a half-way house for the smugglers of times gone by.

Not so very long gone by, however. The " last smuggler " had died in the Lewes work-house not more than a quarter of a century ago. Tales of the " jolly gentleman " were still told. The " haunted tomb " in the church-yard was still avoided by the village folk as though the yarn of the smuggler's ghost, which was supposed to emerge from there and cross the Down at stated periods, was really founded on fact. But whether the ghost tales were true or not, the " Smugglers' Tea-Cosy " was picturesque enough in its solitude to appear the centre of half a hundred legends of the countryside. Even its scarlet signboard, disclosing its anachronistic name so plainly that all who ran might read—even its announce-ment that *teas* and *minerals* were to be had by thirsty wayfarers—could not take away its atmosphere. It stood, wind-swept by the breezes of the Downs, a brave little relic of days gone by.

" Maddy, may we break ranks ? " A perfect chorus broke from the Lower School crocodile.

" *Mais oui, mes enfants. Si vous*——"

But the completion of her sentence was blown to the winds. They were off. At the first sound of her smiling affirmative, laughing, racing, and chasing as light-heartedly as ever did young Lochinvar, the juniors raided the cottage.

" Bags I the biggest packet of Velma."

" Molly, *if* you take all the whip-cream walnuts this time, you'll——"

It mattered little that tuck-boxes from home still held quantities of sweets up at school. To buy goodies at the " Tea-Cosy " on the first Saturday of term was a time-honoured custom, beloved both of the younger Beech Treesites and of Mary Hinnigan herself.

She came to the door to meet them, her Irish eyes gay with delight. " Sure now, an' ef I wasn't after saying last week to the chocolate traveller man when he came——"

" Hullo, Mary. We're back, you see ! The top of the morning to you, Mary ! We're as hungry as hunters. *Have* you got any more of those scrumptious chocolate-ice bars you had last term ? "

" Sure now, I'll be looking round, Miss Mona."

Probably it was as well that Mademoiselle was in indulgent mood. No other mistress would have allowed such a scrimmage. But the scrimmage nature of the shopping expedition was the greatest part of the fun—to Mary Hinnigan as well as to the girls.

" Just help yersilfs, young ladies, and pay me afterwards. It's all one."

Inside the cottage, then, a happy pandemonium reigned, while outside only Josy and Sally waited, accompanied by Mademoiselle, seated on a stone.

" *Jo-see, vous avez l'air triste !* Are you not, zen, hongree, *ma chère? Et vous aussi, Sally ; vous n'avez pas faim ?* "

" It isn't that, Ma'm'selle." Josy stood first on one foot and then on the other, while her eyes scanned the landscape. But in spite of the fact that the gaze of both girls was fixed on the road, the kindly little French lady imagined them both to be acting the part of peris outside Paradise for want of sufficient pocket-money, and hastened to repair the omission.

" You will go in, then, Josee, *n'est-ce pas ?* " She drew a half-crown from her purse. " And you will buy a beeg, beeg, *beeg* packet of *ce chocolat de Suisse, et nous trois nous le mangerons, en plein air,*" she smiled.

This was dreadful. Josy was forced to obey. Sally, in dread silence, remained outside. *How* to part with the letter !

For no possibility did there seem of the appearance of either Perry or Pollitt. As she stood there, with Mademoiselle unconsciously acting gaoler at her side, Sally felt at her wits'

end. At school, before they had started off
that afternoon, everything had seemed possible. Now the letter which had travelled
down in her sports coat pocket seemed certain
to travel back again in the same position. It
would be ridiculous to attempt to ask help
from Mary Hinnigan, who was like a queen
bee among a hive of admirers as she stood in
the midst of the persistent shoppers. Josy
was gone even, and was " taking ages over it,"
so it seemed to Sally. And even Mademoiselle
was looking at her watch and peering within
the little shop door.

" *Mais, maintenant, dépêchez vous, mesdemoi-
selles.*"

It was at that instant that Josy, bright-eyed,
raced suddenly out. " Ma'm'selle, oh Ma'm'-
selle, may I—*puis-je*, I mean. Mary Hinnigan
says that it's in a cage-thing just behind
the house. (Oh, bother, I *can't* say it in
French !) "

" *Eh bien, Jo-see ?* "

" A pigeon, Ma'm'selle. May Sally and I ?
We won't be long. May we ? Oh, I'll say
it all in French afterwards." Twelve-year-old
Josy stamped in her eagerness.

" *Mais oui, mais oui, ma petite.*"

" Oh, *merci*—most awfully *merci*, Ma'm'-
selle." Josy was off.

Sally followed her, her eyes wide with amazement.

" *O-oh !* Sally, there *is* a pigeon. I was in there buying Ma'm'selle's chocs., and I heard her say it. The boys have been. And this pigeon is one of theirs, she says. It came into her garden, tired, and she's letting it rest. She's going to let it fly again this afternoon. Oh, Sally, it's the very thing ! " Josy capered with glee.

" But I don't see," began Sally. For once her ideas didn't keep pace with Josy's.

" Here, give us the letter," chirped Josy, " and we'll tie it on ! Don't you see ? Under its wing—I know the way. I've seen our gardener-boy at home, and helped him. We'll send off your letter *that* way ! Isn't it a lark ? "

It was a lark, too, to both of them when, later on, they reached the ridge of the Down again with the rest of the school, to turn on their chocolate-munching homeward way and watch the unconscious Mary open the cage which they had just left, and lift out the bird. Three times it wheeled above her head, and then it flew over the little wood.

" *Josy,*" said Sally, " I'd *never* have thought of it. Now everything's all right. Sybil ! I don't care a snap for her—not a snap ! " Sally danced a two-step in her glee. "*Now* tell me the ghost tales," she said. "I'll listen to them all the way home, if you like, but I bet I'll tell you worse ones in the dorm. after lights out to-night!"

CHAPTER VIII

SALLY ACTS THE SPOOK

" YES, what *do* they do ? " inquired Sally with interest.

Saturday night had proved rather a disappointment in one kind of way, for it appeared that the rules which she had intended to break could not be broken. All dorm. occupants were actually allowed, at Beech Trees, to talk in bed !

" Always on Saturday nights. Rather. And the prefects don't go to bed till ten that night, ever. I say, I do wonder what they do downstairs all that time," remarked Hesther, undressing.

" Why, yes. We can tell you as many ghost yarns as you like to-night, Sally," remarked Sheila genially, being under the impression that the fresher was " settling in." Last night's visit to Sybil had done the trick, Sheila fondly told herself. Now there would be no more trouble ahead, for Sally had seemed

quite silent and subdued since then until to-
night. It was really rather jolly to have her
cheerier and jollier again, now that Saturday
night had come. During dancing in the Hall,
which was a Saturday feature at Beech Trees,
she had seemed gayer than any one, and everybody had wanted her as partner. Even now,
as she reached the dorm., her eyes were flashing
and sparkling as though she had decidedly
enjoyed her day. Sheila little guessed the
reason of Sally's change of mood.

" Yes ; what *do* the prefects do ? " inquired
she, brushing out her locks. " Private suppers,
I suppose. And as to ghost tales, why, Josy
has been telling me screeds of them all the
way home from the Downs."

" I only told you the ' Haunted Tomb,' "
put in Josy at once. " I hadn't time for the
' Hidden Ways.' And the prefects—well, I
know what they're doing to-night anyhow,
because when I was just finishing washing my
hands Hilda was taking duty, and Louise came
in and told her."

" What ? " everybody wanted to know.

" They're drawing up the fire practice lists,
and having a fire practice meeting. That's it,"
said Josy. " And Meg Fraser, who was washing her hands with me, heard too. She says
we'll have a fire practice almost at once, sure.

She says her dorm.'s noticed that always, directly the officers hold a meeting, we always get an alarm."

" A how-much ? " inquired Sally with interest.

" An alarm. And you'd better know about them, I rather think, if you don't already," put in Sheila, " unless you want to be frightened into fits by that awful bell. First time I heard it I shan't forget. It's quite close to this dorm., you see ; the others don't hear it so loud. Talk of the Seven Sleepers ! Oh yes ; we have dry fire practices every week, Sally. Not wet ones often, though—passing buckets, you know, and all that."

" We go down the fire-escape sometimes," put in Josy. " Once I went down head first for a lark."

" And didn't you catch it ? But we don't have fire-escape drill in the night, you goose," Sheila reminded her. " It's night I'm telling Sally about. I'm in the reserve, and I'll be an officer next year. But Meg Fraser's perfectly right ; I noticed that myself. We do get an alarm practice jolly soon—always after their first meeting. Barbara is head, and she seems simply unable to resist the first chance."

" What's the bell to do with it ? " inquired Sally interestedly.

" Sounds the alarm, of course. We used to have a fire-rattle, but the bell summons the girls quicker—that's what Miss Dean says ; so it's been changed. That huge bell it is, Sally, at the top of the main staircase. Everybody has got to cut and run the instant they hear it. In the night, or any time. Once it was in the middle of Monsieur Sivalli's singing-class, and he simply ramped."

" We had fire drill on board ship coming over," nodded Sally. " It was jolly fun."

" It was more than that the day we had the real fire," put in Sheila, " though not one of us knew till after. Only the captain of the brigade —not even the rest of the officers. The laundry went ablaze, and we suddenly heard the bell. We were rather sick in the Fourths— I was a Fourth then—for we were having lit. with Miss Webb, and were awfully keen. All the same we had to scoot—mistresses too—on to the lawns, where we always go. Then Miss Dean called the roll. It wasn't till after she'd called it, and given a most terrible speech to two girls who'd stayed up in a music-room to finish a duet they were playing, that one of us knew there was a real fire going on, and that the brigade was on the way."

" I say, what a lark," remarked Sally.

" There were some rather footling girls here

then, who'd have been sure to faint away, or
something, if they'd known. Well, they didn't
know, so all was serene. Maisie and Truda
Bratt—they've left now."

" *I*'d have felt funkish if I'd known," put in
Josy quickly.

" I wouldn't." Sally jumped into bed. " I
rather like, personally, to have a squint at
danger. I know I should. Things like snakes
and ghosts, and— Oh, I say, that reminds me.
What *are* those Hidden Ways you talked about ?
They sounded jolly and weird."

The story of the Hidden Ways was as
interesting as its name.

" It's all to do with the smugglers," said
Sheila. " There used to be heaps of them.
Every man was a smuggler in a sort of way, or
winked at it, and got a keg for his pains. The
"Smugglers' Tea-Cosy " is awfully old, and it
was the half-way house for the smugglers coming
up from the coast. It was a farm, and they'd
change horses there without a word and drive
on. There were fights on the Downs sometimes between the land-smugglers and the
revenue officers. Not that there weren't fights
in the Channel too while the goods were being
brought over ; and Miss Todd—she's awfully
keen on the history of the county—*she* says
that the land-smugglers, who didn't really get

much out of it, ran far greater dangers than the
seamen who just left the whisky or silks, or
whatever they brought, and then went back."

" But the Hidden Ways ? " said Sally.

" They're really ripping because they're *real*.
The ghosts were jolly well invented, of course,
by the smugglers themselves, to account for the
noises they made, and to frighten the villagers
from looking out of the windows at them.
But the Hidden Ways really were hidden roads
they used to take right over the Downs.   Miss
Todd has found them."

" I say, I'd like to, too," remarked Sally.

" You'd find it jolly hard to get into them
But one of the girls once did find an entrance,
while we were all out on a picnic.   And of
course the country people know about them,
though they never go near them.   They used
to be just lanes ages ago, you know, before there
were proper roads over the Downs.   And then
everybody used them and they weren't hidden
at all.

" But they got forgotten when the roads were
made ; and Miss Todd—she's awfully keen on
geology being mixed up with geog.—*she* says
that the sandy soil round about here made it
easier for the roads to get washed down.   That's
how they got deeper down, and sort of hollow.
And then it's supposed that the smugglers

bettered that and deepened them to use as a hidden pathway. They look just like masses of bushes with, perhaps, a sheep-track near. But they say that if you follow the sheep-track there's room for a man to ride on horseback for miles and miles and never see the light of day at all."

" *Ride !* O-o-o-oh ! " Sally sat up. " I'm taking riding. I made Granny let me. I adore it. I bet I'll go riding down the Hidden Ways."

" You can safely bet you won't then," put in Sheila. " Josy, there, learns riding. She's the only one in this dorm. that does. She'll tell you that Mr. Baker, the riding-master, is as keen on rules as— I say, that reminds me—" Sheila broke off. " We're not supposed to talk after 9.45, and it's close on that now."

But Sally, though she'd certainly been more than a little interested in the smuggler yarns, was certainly not inclined to consider Sheila in the light of mentor as well as temporary entertainer. The dorm. head's last disparaging remark had served to rekindle her desire for notoriety at any cost.

" No riding-master or any one else is going to bully *me* with his rules," remarked she, " as he'll find out. I'll jolly well find those Hidden Ways if I want to. And, talking of rules, I'm not going to turn over and sleep to order like a baby in a cradle. I'll—" She sat up, quite aware of a sudden bristling interest in the dorm., as shown by an excited rustling from the beds of Hesther and Dorothy.

"Talk of ghosts," continued Sally easily. "Let's have a ghost's patrol, eh? And meet the prefects coming up to bed, and make them turn and run!"

"I tell you what"—Sheila tried the wrong way again—"if you *do*, I'll jolly well report you to Sybil straight bang off."

"Report, is it?" Sally nimbly sprang from her bed. "*There's* an inducement!"

She hadn't really intended to do this particular thing until this instant. She wasn't sure how she was going to do it exactly. Still Sheila's remark had left no doubt in her mind as to one thing: she was going to do it now! The dorm. head, secure in her certainty that the magic of Sybil's lecture would hold good for ever, had perhaps tried too heady a tone.

"Who else is coming? Let's have a long, *long trail-l-l* of ghosts," suggested Sally enticingly to the beds.

There was no reply. "O-o-o-oh, Sal-lee!" seemed to half-flutter in the air from two corners. Sheila, half-impatiently, turned over.

"Stow it, you idjut. Get back to bed.

You'll catch it hot if you do go. But you're just swanking."

"Swanking! You'll see. Idjut, am I? You can jolly well stow your airs. Be head here to anybody in this dorm. who's worm enough to stand it! I don't care a tap for prefects. But I'll jolly well make them care for *me!* If you're all too funkish to come I'll go alone." Sally, with excited eager fingers, was tearing off her sheets. "Where's my gamp? I'll hold it up over my head with the sheet on top. *Now!* D'you not all want to come out and see your beloved Sybil turn and run?"

"Sally, don't!" It was Josy's voice in an urgent kind of gasp.

But Sally, looking imposing enough certainly, garbed as she was in white, and looming tall and spectre-like with the aid of the umbrella over which sheet-folds hung down in draperies as far as her toes, had certainly no intention of giving in.

"'Don't,' is it? You'd better come yourself, Josy! I wouldn't funk if I were you. Pooh! I'd rather be afraid of spooks than prefects."

Sally was gone. Down the passage with a whirl and whisk of spectre-like draperies.

"*Well-l-l!*" Sheila sat up in bed. "I didn't

really think she meant it. And there's the clock striking ten. What *am* I supposed to do ? I jolly well wish she'd stayed in India. I wish she'd go back there. I wish any one had got her in their dorm. but me. The prefects always come up most awfully punc., too. And——"

She stopped short suddenly with a gasp, and sprang like lightning from her bed, for a sudden and unexpected sound seemed almost to shake the room.

CHAPTER IX

AN UNOFFICIAL FIRE-DRILL

"CLANG-G-G ! Clang-g-g-g-g ! Clang-g-g-g-g-g-g-g !!! "

Sleeping girls, just entering upon their first dreams, sat up in bed. " Bother ! oh, *bother !* The fire-bell ! "

There was no doubt about that. It *was* the fire-alarm. Every one of them knew the brazen stand-no-waiting clang. In three minutes every member of the household was due to be on the lawn outside the school, or to merit fines and worse. Every one must pass down the corridor to the main stairway and then down to the front door below in orderly file. There must be no speaking in the passages *en route*. So ran the fire brigade rules which all girls knew by heart. But as they flew into their dressing-gowns there was time for speculation.

" Is it a real fire ? O-o-oh ! it must be ; coming in the middle of the night like this ! "

" The lawn ! We'll *never* have a midnight meeting there for roll-call, will we ? "

" Shut up there. Stow terrifying the kids. Buck up and *go !* that's all you're told to do." Thus the urgent tones of the dorm. heads, who must act captain and be the last to stick to the mataphorical ship.

Pad, pad, pad, in slippered feet the girls began to sally forth. In Sheila's dorm., too, arrangements had gone on as per schedule.

" Here, Hesther and Dorothy, show a leg. No, leave your purse behind, you silly kid, and come. What *am* I to do about Sally ? And, Josy, come back. Why on earth——" She spoke in a distracted air while hunting for a shoe.

" I'm just going outside to bring her back," announced Josy from the door.

" Come back, then, I say. I jolly well tell you that I'm not going to have *you* starting Sally's tricks," called her head. But Josy had gone.

Somehow she couldn't stay. Somehow she had to go. She had a sudden hope that Sally, who had departed so very soon before the clanging began, might, perhaps, under cover of the excitement that prevailed, consent to return and doff her ghostly apparel and become as other girls, thereby saving herself from the " most awful row." Josy meant to try to induce Sally to do this. If she could, why, the hated fire-alarm was a godsend. She would do her best. She went to do it. Pad, pad. It was Josy's soft-slippered feet which reached the stair-top first.

" *Oh !* " Josy stood stock-still, staring. She had not expected this. For there, under the great bell, stood Sally herself. At first Josy's heart, too, stood still with horror. This was worse than ghosts, worse than anything that the school could imagine. This was terrible. For Sally, so it appeared, Sally herself, was ringing and ringing at the bell.

Clang ! Clang-g-g ! Clang-g-g-g-g ! it went. Then *Cl-l-lang !* in feverish haste. Then came a sudden silence. Then suddenly, while Josy stood still, transfixed with horror to the spot, there came the still small voice. Still and small, and unlike Sally's usual tones, but it *was* Sally's voice

" Josy, I'm *caught* to this wretched bell— my hateful gamp that I'm dressed up with. *Oh !* "

Then came a most tremendous and terrifying clanging, followed by the sudden collapse of Sally ; in a garment of white draperies and an armour of umbrella ribs she sank gracefully on to the corridor floor.

" At last ! " panted she half-sobbingly.

It was *then* that the prefects arrived—up the stairs, half a dozen steps at a time.

The whole affair had taken, perhaps, a minute and a half. Up the stairs they all flew. *This* was no prearranged alarm, as each of them, well in the know, realized : unless something dire and dreadful had occurred.

" Who's there ? Who's ringing the bell ? What's up ? " Barbara, head girl of the school, captain of the cricket, captain, too, of the hockey team, captain of the fire brigade—to give her some of her titles—reached the top stair first.

" It's me and Sally," chirped Josy's voice as bravely as it could speak, while at that instant, pad, pad, pad, up the corridors in stealthy, sober haste came lines of girls, each with their dorm. head bringing up the rear, *en route*, sans question, for the front lawn in the middle of the night.

" *You* rang the bell ? " The captain's voice was unbelieving. " May I ask how, and why ? "

" For—a lark," came a muffled sound from beneath a pile of sheets.

" Left, right." The captain's voice had boomed forth before the words were hardly uttered. It was not for nothing that Barbara was head girl of Beech Trees. " Carry on, all.

Downstairs to the corridor. Sybil and Phyllis, will you take command, please ? Dry practice indoors."

There had not been an instant's pause. The stream filed down the stairs, true to discipline. But every one of them had to pass Sally's huddled heap as they went. Now she was *truly* famous, if this was fame !

" And now—" The captain's voice spoke out, crisp and clear, when the procession had disappeared and when the professional tones of the brigade officers below could be heard enunciating their orders, " *Pass-s-s !* Left. *Pass* buckets—*right !* "—" And now, will you explain the matter, if you please ? "

" Barbara, she didn't mean to. Not *that* part of it, she didn't, really. Honest Injun," Josy burst in in a perturbed and shaking voice, though she stood her ground steadily at Sally's side. She hardly knew why she had stayed. But somehow she had felt that there was nothing else to be done. Sally was in a pickle, so she couldn't leave her, not possibly. " Barbara, honest Injun——"

" Josy "—the head girl looked down—" kindly keep to facts. How could that possibly be ? And will you, please, allow Sally to speak for herself ? " Barbara spoke in a freezing tone.

Josy had never been spoken to like this

before. Of little " rows " she had had full experience. She had always been a pickle, but—though she didn't know it—a very lovable pickle indeed, against whom nobody among either the prefects or the mistresses had a hard word to say. Her escapades had been of the " light-hearted order," according to her form-mistress ; " *cette chérie*, Josie," was Mademoiselle's pet name for her. She had never been insubordinate ; she had never broken rules except by mistake, and then she had been most terribly and truly contrite. Barbara, the captain, had always seemed to Josy the embodiment of all heroic qualities ; every prefect had seemed to her to be as impressive in deed and truth as they all honestly tried to be. To the mistresses Josy lifted eyes of fearful admiration ; to Miss Dean, the Head, she had never yet raised her voice above a whisper. And in her heart there was a tremendous love and reverence for " school " and everything that Beech Trees meant. She loved everything and everybody there in much the same way as she loved home.

But there was a new way of loving growing now in Josy's heart. She somehow loved Sally differently.

Sally was big ; years and years older than Josy. But Sally was " little " in some ways, as Josy somehow felt, though she hadn't voiced that idea, and would have wondered at herself if she had really known how she felt. Sally appealed to that part of Josy's heart which had, before school days, given itself to certain dolls who were supposed to be " afraid of the dark and things like that, but *very* brave," and so were allowed to sleep, for comfort and company, under the pillow of their mistress night after night, while well-dressed beauties sat in the toy-cupboard and braved the night alone.

For the Sally of their first meeting, when the look in the new girl's eyes had reminded Josy of that hunted frightened wild thing trying to hold its own and to keep its pride in spite of its fears, could never be quite forgotten. It had been a look the more piteous for the poise of Sally's proud head just then. Josy had never heard the word "piteous"; she only knew that Sally was different, somehow, from anybody she had known before. In some strange way she seemed small Josy's special charge !

And when Sally had adopted Josy as her only companion in all the world of girls at Beech Trees, Josy's heart felt strangely glad. For Sally was wonderful, wonderful in her daring ; Josy admired her, even her faults. The love for Beech Trees, and everybody and everything concerned, was deep in Josy's heart ; but somehow Sally had, in her way, wrought a change.

Hence, for the first time, Josy had disobeyed her dorm. head knowingly; for the first time she stood facing the captain and daring—yes, daring—to speak up for Sally the words that she knew Sally was too proud to say.

"Is this true what Josy says, that you rang the bell *by mistake?* Kindly get up and explain." There was scorn in Barbara's voice; there was scorn in Barbara's eye as she gazed down at the huddled mass at her feet.

"I'm perfectly willing, except that my feet are wound round with sheets. I was having a lark, I repeat," remarked Sally, struggling up. "Josy wasn't in it at all."

"Josy?" Barbara turned.

"I was. I was. I mean I *did* break rules, and meant to. Barbara, truly—" began Josy hastily.

CHAPTER X

—AND ITS CONSEQUENCES

" I HOPE you're as sick with yourself as you deserve to be," remarked Sheila grimly.

It was the day after the false fire-alarm, and if Sally had meant to make her mark in the school, her wish had certainly been granted in full.

" Here am I," continued Sheila, " called up by Sybil and "—she donned her Sunday headgear lugubriously—" and told that I can't manage a dorm. I jolly well could if I'd got anybody else in it but you, Sally. Hesther and Dorothy don't make asses of themselves and bring down tons of bricks on other people's heads. And Josy's been absolutely all right always till this term. Now it seems she's taking a leaf out of your rotten book. Josy, you'd have kept out of the row absolutely if you'd stayed in here last night when I told you, and come downstairs with us. As it is——"

" Perhaps she didn't want to," put in Sally serenely. But her face was rather patched.

" You can just shut up, Sally, with your airs. I tell you plainly I'm sick of them. There's no girl at Beech Trees thinks you anything but an ass for tearing them out of their beds last night. Perhaps you don't realize that Josy's never been had up by Barbara before, and to my mind it's not a thing she deserves. I hated to say so, but as she *did* bunk out——"

" I went on my own. It wasn't Sally's fault ; it was mine. Honest Injun, it was," put in Josy's small voice, rather shakily.

She had just returned from Barbara's room, where she had had the first real rowing of her young life. Last night the captain had dismissed her to bed almost at once, and she had been lying there with her head under the sheets when the others returned grumbling from the fire practice. Sally herself had not returned to the dorm. that night. Straight to Miss Dean's study Barbara had hied her, in her warpaint and just as she was. And that part of the punishment had been to Sally very real indeed. She had stood in full view of the Head, and, incidentally, in full view of herself also, as imaged in the mirror on the opposite wall she saw herself looking as utterly foolish as a girl could look.

" Will you explain, Sara ? "

Miss Dean had looked her up and down It was difficult to be brisk and Sally-ish and to ape an air of *savoir-faire* when facing the glint of amusement in the headmistress's steady eyes, and while facing, also, that lunatic image of herself just behind.

" It was just a lark," Sally muttered angrily.

" A lark ? Rather a poor one, I think. Its results will last longer, I fear, my dear, than any fun you may have derived from it. Look at those sheets. Of course they will have to be mended by you."

Sally looked down at the long long rips and strips. She hated and detested needles and thread and anything to do with sewing.

" From your own bed ? Well, of course, you will not sleep there to-night. Not for some little while I think, since you seem not to realize that you are upsetting the comfort of others there." The headmistress spoke in a level, quiet, and business-like tone. She did not seem one bit perturbed nor amazed. Then her voice changed a little. " And, Sara——"

" Yes." Sally's face was growing rather blank beneath its smears and smuts. She hadn't anticipated being put to sleep elsewhere. She would miss the rest, especially Josy. Also that wretched sheet.

" Sara, it seems that you *never* consider any-body's comfort but your own ? "

Miss Dean seemed to wait for a reply.

" No, I don't think I do," said Sally, half-defiantly.

" There we are agreed then. No, *I* do not think you do either. Well, that is something we must work from here. Suppose every-body behaved as you have behaved to-night, Sara ? "

A sudden gleam came into Sally's eyes.

" It would be a bit of a lark."

" Exactly, my dear. *Your* kind of lark, you mean. Do you know whose sentiments, almost exactly, you are expressing ? "

" Whose ? " Sally didn't understand.

" You don't ? Those of a Bolshevist." Miss Dean's voice was deliberate. " A Bolshevist, you see, Sara. And a Bolshevist who is really an enemy of his country. No advancement can there be while he persists, or she persists, in his, or her, *utterly selfish* way. Suppose we *did* all decide to behave like Bolshevists, well, temporarily a Bolshevist country might, perhaps, consider itself, to use your own ex-pression, ' having a lark.' But Britishers think differently."

" *I'm* British." Sally held up her head.

" Exactly, Sara. Well, please do not, by

your behaviour, lead the others to question that fact, will you ? "

Sally suddenly found herself dismissed, the remembrance of the Head's last remark still in her ears, in the cold incisive tone that she had not heard Miss Dean use before. Dismissed up to the San., too, where Matron absolutely flared up like tinder at the sight of her sheets and would hear no speech from Sally, her own flow of indignant words continuing until the delinquent was in bed.

" Into that bed you get ; it's Miss Dean's orders. And in here you sleep every night until those sheets are mended, and properly mended. Mis-using other people's property. Have you had any one to bring you up, eh, or *not* ? Heathen native ways ; that's what I call this kind of thing. We've had other girls here from India who didn't play silly tricks like *this* ! Do you think the school fees cover playing hanky-panky with the school sheets ? for if you do, you're wrong. It's lucky you'll be if you get through the darning of these by sitting at them all next Saturday afternoon. There'll be no holiday for you. And here you sleep every night until your own bed linen is ready for your bed again, and that's *that* ! "

Sally's ears were burning, and her eyes felt burning, too, as she hastened into bed and tried to hide from Matron's scathing tongue beneath the clothes.

" Native ways," had she ? A "Bolshevist," was she ? The expressions fairly pricked her in her most vulnerable spot—her pride. Straight home from India as she was, proud in every bit of her of every drop of her British blood, and with a thoroughly British feeling for all things native-born, owing to the surroundings in which she had been brought up, Sally could hardly bear Matron's last speech.

" Dad would be sick with me for them saying it," she thought. " Bother ! After all, it *was* just a lark ; and I *am* British, and I needn't care." But, just as Miss Dean had said, somehow the lark didn't seem worth while now, considering the bothers that it had already brought—bothers that weren't over yet by any means. For the sheets were waiting to be darned next half-holiday ; there was every expectation of sleeping alone in the dreary San. under the Matron's eye for a week at least. And what had happened to Josy she wouldn't know till next day anyhow. " I hope the kid didn't get into a row," thought Sally as she went to sleep.

Next day brought further humiliation. Sheila's frank and uncompromising expressions of distaste ; stony looks from half the school ;

particularly crisp tones from the mistresses. Sally would have felt lonely, indeed, but for Josy, who hovered continually all through Sunday at her side.

Josy had been called up by Barbara, and had stood facing the head girl, a very small and straight twelve-year-old with a patch of crimson colour in the middle of each cheek, and one foot eagerly pawing the ground.

" Josy, Sheila reported you for breaking rules after the alarm went."

" Yes, Barbara."

" Josy, you must keep rules, you know."

" Ye-es, Barbara."

" For what would happen to Beech Trees if we didn't, Josy ? "

" Oh, I will, Barbara. But——"

" But there mustn't be any ' buts '; that's why you're here, for me to tell you so. We can't pick and choose the rules we'll keep ; none of us. Now you can go, but remember." Barbara's speech was very short and very simple, and suitable for a very junior girl.

But Josy came away feeling, for the first time in her life since she had arrived at Beech Trees, most unaccountably unhappy. There *was* a " but," she told herself. Perhaps Barbara didn't understand. Josy, for the first time, found herself realizing that there was a part of her growing different somehow; a part of her that felt new. She loved Beech Trees terribly, most terribly, she told herself; till now it wouldn't have occurred to her to break any rule on purpose, though she had done so sometimes without meaning to, of course, and had been dreadfully sorry afterwards. But last night things had been different. Since Sally had come things had been growing different. And she didn't see her way clear at all. Yesterday, after the alarm went, she hadn't obeyed Sheila and she hadn't stayed in the dorm. when she had been ordered to do so, because she *did* so want Sally to get safely back and miss a " row." If she had obeyed Sheila, of course, and had gone down with the rest, she'd never have been called up by Barbara, and that was a disgrace which she must tell Mummy about when she wrote home.

Which ought she to have done ? She didn't exactly know. She only knew that things didn't seem so easy to her as to Barbara. " Obey orders, and no ' buts,' " Barbara had said. Well, perhaps—Josy walked slowly and rather sadly along the corridor towards her dorm., thinking as she went. But as she passed along, thinking, Josy remembered that first day of term, and Sally's face. She remembered Sally, too, big girl though she was, sobbing in bed, and not minding Josy hearing, though nobody else might know. Sally had said "You *do* count." And even while she was remembering Josy knew that she *did*.

It was at that instant that she caught the sounds of talking from one of the open dorm. doors, where others besides her own dorm. mates towards whom she was hurrying were donning church apparel.

"That Sally Heath's absolutely the limit. She's turned out of her dorm., they say. It serves her right. If she thinks she's going to amaze Beech Trees by a silly trick like last night's she's mistaken. All the girls say they won't——"

The voices died down as Josy passed on. But suddenly Josy knew that she couldn't do anything else but stand by Sally. If all the Beech Trees girls gave Sally the cold shoulder she simply couldn't help it.

"I truly think there are more 'buts' about rules than Barbara thinks there are," thought small Josy wistfully.

CHAPTER XI

SALLY MAKES A PLAN

" ISN'T it detestable, Josy? And there's another just as big!" Sally made a grimace at her through a rent in a sheet.

A week had gone by—a hateful week so far as Sally's opinion was concerned, although by any other member of Beech Trees the term was considered to be just as jolly as usual.

Games were in full swing now that the term was well begun. Mistresses were fairly embarked on their various syllabuses of favourite subjects for the session. Special instructors had recommenced their weekly visits to Beech Trees once more ; and consequently swimming, riding, fencing, and dancing lessons were the topics of enthusiasts in the free hours which fell to their lot.

No free hours had Sally. Matron had seen to that. A pillow-case seemed to haunt her steps—after the manner of the ghost it had once helped to suggest—from Monday to Wednesday

of the week. On Thursday, after a scathing
lecture from Matron, a large torn sheet took its
place.

"You'll keep this in your locker, Sally—just
as you've kept the pillow-slip till it was mended ;
and neatly folded, please, in paper. Remember,
it will go on your bed again. You'd only used
it two nights, and you'll finish out the week
like other girls better-mannered than yourself.
Why should *you* be treated different, I ask you ?
Yes, well then, you'll keep this in your locker,
and you'll take it out when you've any spare
time, and you'll darn it. And better than the
pillow-slip was darned, I hope and trust. And
you'll not go back to sleep in your dormitory
again till this sheet and the other sheet are
ready."

Sally, realizing that she truly *must* work out
her own salvation from the dreary San., the only
alleviation from whose boredom was a spirited
nightly lecture from Matron on her behaviour,
had set to work on her bed linen with a docility
more reminiscent of a fairy princess imprisoned
in a long-ago dungeon than of Sara Heath.

But the prospect of release from the San.
was not the only reason of her industry. Sally
was thankful, in a way, of something to do in
odd moments, even sheet-mending, to cover
up the fact that just now she was practically

at Coventry so far as the rest of the Beech Trees girls were concerned. Nobody wanted to have more than was absolutely necessary to do with her; nobody sought her out in any way whatever. She was taboo.

On the first few days of her life at school things had been very different. Sally had seemed "a bit bumptious" in the eyes of everybody, but everybody had expected her to settle down. On the first Saturday night, during dancing in Hall, Sally had had as many partners as she could wish. She had had her brief reign, too, over Hesther and Dorothy at any rate, in the dormitory; and in class, her companions, being younger than she was, had been inclined to treat her with a certain deferential friendliness.

But since Saturday night everything was changed. In the opinion of Beech Trees Sally, an absolute fresher, had actually tried to "take a rise" out of the whole school. She had even, to a certain extent, been successful, since she had roused every girl, and had indirectly inaugurated a fire practice which would not have fallen to their lot unless she had rung the alarm-bell. If Sally had owned up that the ringing was the mistake that it really was, that the lark was "just a dressing-up lark," the result of her escapade would have been different.

Certainly there would have been a " row,"
but the " row " would have cleared the air of
the whole affair.

But she had not owned to this, for very
vanity and pride she had not wanted to own
up that the wild and feverish clanging was due
to nothing more nor less than the fact that
part of her ghostly rig-up had become attached
to the bell-rope and wouldn't detach itself for
all her efforts. And so the whole school,
except Josy, was under the impression that the
new girl had dared to set out to play a trick
on them all, and that she probably thought she
had scored.

The dignity of Beech Trees had been attacked,
therefore Sally must be made to understand
that such a thing would not be tolerated—that
a girl who behaved in this kind of way was,
pro tem. at any rate, an outsider. Later on,
of course, when she understood her position in the school, things would be different. Such was the universal opinion of Beech
Trees.

Up in the dorm.—for Sally " changed " there
during the daytime as usual—Sheila spoke out
her mind now, knowing that she had the whole
school to back her up. Hesther and Dorothy
were engaged in " talking games " nowadays,
and had no time for listening for any brilliant

repartee from Sally. In class, too, Sally felt
more or less of an Ishmael, because, though
every one was quite polite, that was all. On
the field she was generally alone ; in walks, if
it hadn't been for Josy, whose walk-times co-
incided with her own, Sally would have been
forced to make the only-tolerated member of a
threesome at the end of the line. Nobody was
in the least rude or unkind to her, but somehow
she seemed unnoticed, which was worse, far
worse, to Sally than to have to listen upstairs
each night to Matron's torrents of disciplinary
advice.

Yes, Sally had had a hateful week. She hated
Beech Trees, so she told herself, more than she
had thought she could have hated any school.
She would far, far rather, only she wouldn't
have owned it, even to herself, have been at
home riding roughshod and ruthlessly over her
grandmother's wishes. If it hadn't been for
small Josy, Sally would have felt Beech Trees
a wilderness indeed.

Josy became really indispensable in those
days. For to Josy still she felt herself a kind
of hero. Josy was as loyal in her champion-
ship as she had ever been. Sally knew, somehow, that she could always be sure of Josy. It
was Josy who, wide-eyed and sympathetic, had
raced feverishly, booted and walk-clad, into the

Common-room on Saturday afternoon where Sally sat alone.

"Sally, good-bye. We're going, you see. Oh, I do most specially wish you were coming too, because "—Josy's words fell out on the top of each other—" it's Miss Gill that's taking us, and we're going on the Downs."

"The Downs?" Sally laid down a lazy needle.

"Yes; to see the dew-pond over the hill. Only a few of us have seen it. And we may find the Hidden Ways. Miss Gill knows one entrance, you know, and she says that we can hunt if we like. And we're going to enter the dew-pond on our Guide maps, and perhaps the Hidden Ways if we find them. But not unless—" Josy stopped for breath.

"That place where horses can ride down unseen?" Sally sprang to attention. "Oh, Josy, I wish I was coming. Who are you walking with, eh?"

"With Miss Gill, at the end. But only just by accident." Josy coloured. "I kept free, Sally, you know, just in case Matron changed round and forgave you the sheet. Hilary and Freda had both asked me; but when I couldn't because of that, then they joined up with each other. And then Judy, who's been booked to Miss Gill since last term, was most awfully

kind, and said she didn't mind if I asked Miss
Gill if I might walk on her other side." Josy
was flushed. She didn't want Sally to understand that she had really spoilt her own pros-
pects of an afternoon's jolly partner by keeping
herself for Sally, just in case the new girl
should be set free.

Sally didn't notice this, however. She was
full of a wild idea. " Then who are you going
to search with ? For the Hidden Ways, I
mean. We'd have searched together if I'd
been coming."

" Rather. But then you're not. Oh, I don't
know. All together, perhaps. Half the girls
will crowd round Miss Gill, of course, when we
break lines. Or with Hilary, perhaps, if she
asks me. We walked together most Saturdays
last term ; but of course she's booked to
Freda now." If there was a glint of disappointment in Josy's bright eye Sally didn't
notice it.

" I say," said Sally. " Good. Then don't
join on to anybody. See ? " She lifted up her
needle and began to work furiously.

" Not anybody ? " repeated Josy, wonder-
ingly.

" No. Do what I tell you, Josy. No, I'm
not going to explain. I know the way you're
taking to the Downs all right. And, by the

way, don't keep too close to the rest. A little
way off, you know. It's stupid, when you're
looking for secret entrances, *I* think, to all go
peering about in a bunch. It would be far
more interesting for you and me to find it
alone."

" You and me ! " repeated Josy, still staring.

" I wish you wouldn't repeat everything I
say," said Sally, her eyes on her darning, which
was rushing along at headlong speed. " Look
here, I'm not going to say another word. Do
as I tell you. See ? " Sally grinned, just as
the sound of steps passed the door in the hall
outside.

" Good-bye. I don't think I understand
quite, but I'll—" said Josy, racing to the door.

" Now, Josy "—Miss Gill's voice sounded
outside—" who gave you leave, I should like
to know, to go into the Common-room in your
brogues ? "

" I was only just saying good-bye to Sally,
Miss Gill," chirped Josy's voice very apologetically.

" Silly kid," muttered the said Sally, bending
over her sheet, and drawing her stitches in and
out with headlong haste.

For Sally had a sudden notion. She wanted
tremendously to see those Hidden Ways.
The idea of riding down a secret passage was

to her, the fearless rider, the possibility of a ripping adventure. She was sick, so she told herself, at missing this chance, and she wasn't going to miss it, unless she must. Matron had certainly declared that her holiday afternoon must be given up to working at the sheets until they were darned. Well, if they *were* darned, Sally told herself, she would be free to go.

She darned away without looking up at all for over half an hour. By this time the girls must be up on the Downs—perhaps already searching. Josy was a regular little sport, and she would do as Sally had told her. Well, she wouldn't have to wait about long now.

Sally, remembering Matron's powers of repartee and love of order, folded her work carefully, returned it to the locker, and put away her scissors before she left the Common-room. Now she had every right to go, she told herself; every right. She hastened down to the empty cloakroom, donned her school hat and her walking shoes, and was off and away as fast as her nimble legs could take her towards the Downs.

CHAPTER XII

THE HIDDEN WAYS

BUT Josy found it rather difficult to follow Sally's orders. For although she herself would not have expressed it so, Josy was tremendously popular. She was recognized at Beech Trees by every one as a little sport, though she was ready enough for mischief. She was full of ideas, too, and very sensible for her age. In short, she was good company and game.

Judy, Miss Gill's special devotee, had not been altogether as unselfish as she might have been had any other junior schoolgirl but Josy been concerned, when she offered the said Josy Miss Gill's unengaged half. For Josy was tactful and fair ; she would realize that school etiquette demanded that Judy should have the lion's share of the mistress under the circumstances. Other girls were not so accommodating as was Josy.

" Stick to Miss Gill when we break lines,

Josy," Judy then adjured her, " or your share
of her will be surrounded, and I shan't get any
good out of my walk at all! Unless "—Judy,
being fair and tactful also, noticed the expression of Josy's open features—" are you
engaged to any one else ? "

" I might—I thought, perhaps, if Hilary,"
mumbled Josy, wondering in a worried way
whether she was fibbing or whether she wasn't.

" Oh, well," said Judy generously, " if it's
Hilary, *go*. I know she's been missing you
this term, for she's in my dorm., and we all
think you're awfully taken up with that new
Sally."

The walk began. Josy was no hindrance
whatever in the conversation, it being chiefly
upon home matters, which Judy poured garrulously into Miss Gill's courteous ears. The
youngest member of the threesome walked
along demurely on the mistress's other side,
feeling rather bothered.

She hadn't fibbed, had she, she asked herself,
about Hilary ? She hadn't meant to, but it
was a fib. Oh, how horribly easy fibs were,
and so hateful. Mummy would hate her to
fib, and Beech Trees never fibbed. She would
tell Judy that. Oh, but she *couldn't*, because
Sally had made her promise. Josy gave a
sigh.

And she *had* been friends with Hilary—best friends. She was dreadfully fond of Hilary still. Hilary had seemed to join up with Freda lately, but Josy knew that it wasn't because Hilary wasn't faithful. It was because Josy had begun always to feel that she must keep free herself in case Sally wanted her. To-day she had almost promised to join on to Hilary at break-ranks, but now she didn't see how she could, because of what Sally had said just at the end. What had Sally meant? Josy sighed again.

" That's sigh number two, Josy," said Miss Gill cheerily, looking down with a smile at the small straight figure at her side, " and two too many for a Saturday afternoon walk! I'm afraid you're not so interested in Judy's family of Belgian hares at home as she and I are. See, there's the ridge where the dew-pond is— right at the top there. Run and tell the rest to race up, and tell them, too, to stay there till I get up; for it's very interesting to hear about, and it's the only dew-pond in this district."

It *was* interesting. Almost as fairy-looking as its name suggested, too, though Miss Gill proceeded to tell them, when she reached the top ridge of the Down, that fairies had nothing to do with its making.

" The mountain dews are supposed to keep the dew-pond full always, year in and year out, in a truly magical way," she said, " when once they have been filled by snow or rain." She leaned over the side of the shallow little cup-shaped pond. " There aren't any dew-ponds in Britain except in our county, you know ; and as one walks over the Downs one comes upon them so suddenly and unexpectedly that they do seem a kind of magic."

" It's most awfully blue, the water, Miss Gill —as blue as the sea."

" As blue as the sky, you mean. It's reflected so well because the shepherds make them on the highest top. It's the shepherds who know the secret of how to make dew-ponds. And only a few of them now—the last few of a long, long line. They're made on the top of a Down, I've heard, because the ridge is generally capped with chalk, you see, and chalk holds the water safely so that it won't sink down into the soil below. That's the secret of a dew-pond. That is why it is always full."

" I wish there was a more fairy-like reason," suggested a voice.

" I expect the sheep are more satisfied than you, Hilary," laughed Miss Gill, " to say nothing of the shepherds. This tiny pool is always ready when the sheep need it just because of that common-sense chalk cap! Still, cheer up. The fairies—or the ' Pharisees,' as the village people call them—are supposed to be fond of bathing in the dew-ponds, I believe, even if they don't invent them."

The girls laughed. It was on the highest ridge of the Down that they were all grouped together. It had taken them nearly an hour to climb up from the school. On one side of them, far below, not near enough for them to hear the sound of its mighty swell, stretched the blue waters of the Channel. Below them lay the village, with the church and the spreading churchyard, and a little way nearer the big red buildings of the school. The playing-fields were plain to see ; the figures of the senior girls could be descried easily enough. On every other side stretched the Down ; soft and billowy in its curves, it seemed all round them.

" There's Shanctonbury Ring," pointed some one.

" I can see three windmills—no, four——"

" No, five—if you count ours just close."

It was a glorious day, blue and green with beauties of sea and land.

" Now, girls, I advise you, while we're here,

to enter the dew-pond on your maps. That's why you asked to come, wasn't it ? "

" Oh, Miss Gill "—every one looked up together—" and then may we try to trace the entrance that you found to the Hidden Ways ? "

For Miss Gill herself had once, during a tramp over the Downs, found an opening into the smugglers' secret road. She had told all the school about it. " Perfectly simple *when you know*, and not difficult to find either. It will be good practice for you on a Guide walk."

The moment seemed to have arrived, certainly thought the girls.

Miss Gill thought so too. " Yes, of course you may. But my entrance is about a mile from here. We might just do it by crossing those ridges and be back for tea. You'd rather find it yourselves, of course ? "

" Oh, Miss Gill, *of course*. *Rather !* "

" Then scoot as fast as you can, all of you. I shall follow on."

It was quite easy, then, for Josy to leave the others. She felt a little bothered about doing so, but she simply had to, she thought, for the obvious reason that, as they had been standing on the dew-pond ridge, while the rest had been trying to distinguish the figures of various seniors on the playing-field, Josy had found her own eyes fixed on something else. Sally—the figure of Sally—was crossing the fence which marked the boundary from the Down, and was coming up their way. Probably she didn't see them, high on the sky-line, but she had crossed a ridge and was on the way higher still before the group turned on the Hidden Ways discovery quest.

" She'll go wrong and miss us," thought Josy. " Miss Gill's way is quite different from the one she's on. I wonder if I could tell Miss Gill and ask her." But it was very difficult to know. Sally had been in so many " rows," thought Josy sadly, and this might mean another. Had she really got Matron's permission to come or not ? " Well, anyhow, she told me not to tell, and that's as good as me promising." Josy sighed. Life seemed growing dreadfully complicated, and it had never been complicated before. She stood wondering.

" Coming, Josy ? " shouted Hilary, racing on ahead with Freda.

Josy paused for a moment and wondered, and decided with a sigh that she *wasn't* coming. She had no real partner, so she wouldn't be missed. Judy would imagine her with Hilary, and Hilary, who was growing used to being without her, would imagine her still with Judy.

Josy slipped down the ridges easily enough towards the direction from which Sally had been seen beginning to climb. She had three ridges to cross before they would meet. There was nobody in view; there was not even the sound of a sheep-bell to be heard. The Downs smelt sweet in the sun; gorse-pods cracked in the heat now and then close by; under her feet little tiny Down plants were growing; the world seemed a lovely place, blue and green with happiness, Josy thought. Everything surely would be right. She would tell Sally that they must keep rules together; she would ask Sally to let her explain to Miss Gill. Everything seemed as though there was nothing to worry about. Why, as Miss Gill said, if fairies lived on the Down and bathed in the dew-ponds, how lovely everything was! Josy began as she ran along to make up a little dew-pond song in her head.

" Bathing in a dew-pond,"

sang Josy to a tune of her own,

" Is the greatest fun !
   But wait till the chill is off
   The dew or you're sure to cough ! "

She gave a little joyous laugh, then she went on :

" And the sound of a fairy's cough, you know,
    Breaks a magic spell made—oh, long ago !—
    A spell on the Down gnomes at Back of
        Beyond,
    Who may never, no, *never*, spy out a dew-
        pond !
    If you cough,
    That spell's *off !* "

" I'll sing that to baby boy when I get home,
if I remember it as long," Josy thought, smiling
to herself. Then suddenly fairies and gnomes
and magic were forgotten. Or *was* it magic ?
For something queer was happening somewhere. Quite near, from the middle of a big
clump of bushes, there rose a curl of white
smoke ! " Why, it's actually exactly like the
Burning Bush that Moses found," thought
Josy. " Or *do* fairies really have fires ? " She
crept up close and peered as near as she
could go.

Then came the second wonderful thing.
Up out of nowhere, so it seemed, there peered
an inquisitive gipsy head—not an ill-natured
face by any means, though certainly a curious
one.

" Oh, I do beg your pardon," said Josy
politely. " I never thought it was *your* fire,
you know. But how——"

" Why, sure, the gentle little rawnee came

upon the poor Romany's camp all unknowing," said the gipsy woman, showing her
teeth in a smile, and still peering up out of
the bushes.

" *Oh !* " cried Josy, staring back and little
by little beginning to understand this strange
phenomenon. " Why, I believe you're standing deep down inside the Hidden Ways ! "

" The Hidden Ways—why, sure, little
rawnee." The gipsy woman made no secret
of it. " And there's more than the track,
little rawnee, that lies hidden from *you*, sure.
But the Romanies know, and if the gentle
rawnee will cross the hand of the poor Romany
with a silver bit she could show——"

" I haven't any silver, I'm sorry." Josy
smiled at her. " But talking of ' showing
things,' I've got a friend here—quite close, I
think—and I would so like to bring her here
to see. She'll love it. Would you show us
your camp in the Hidden Ways ? " Josy broke
off.

" Why, sure, little gentle rawnee," began
the woman kindly enough.

" Sally ! *Sal-lee !* SALLY ! " shouted Josy
in great excitement, making a trumpet of her
small hands. " *Sara Heath !* *Coo-eee !* "

A strange thing happened then, though Josy
didn't see it. The woman's face, which had

looked disappointed at Josy's first reply, suddenly lighted up as the girl uttered Sally's name. An intent look crept into her eyes, and they suddenly flashed. She turned round suddenly, and disappeared from view.

CHAPTER XIII

THE LETTER AGAIN

" I'M sure she was here," panted Josy. "Just a moment ago. Yes, there's the smoke."

" I say," said Sally with interest. She had been making her way up over the green hummocks of the wide Down when she had heard Josy's call, and she had raced to meet her. "Coo-eee! Here-oh! Jo-seee!" she had shouted enthusiastically. For it had been more than jolly suddenly to hear her name called out in the younger girl's excited friendly little pipe. Sally had been feeling rather grim and vindictive about things in general and school in particular as she raced over the turf.

She hated Beech Trees, she told herself. Had she broken one of their rules in escaping as she had done? Well, perhaps. But she wasn't going to care. Matron had said she was to stick indoors till the sheets were finished—well, they were finished now, in a way, and so here she was. Now she meant to keep her weather-eye cocked for Josy's solitary figure. " I told her to keep apart from the rest," thought Sally. " I really detest every one of them, and if she were joined on it wouldn't be easy perhaps to unjoin her. Besides, with all these wretched rules about, if Miss Gill were to see me——"

Sally's hand was against every one's save that of Josy just then, and therefore the sound of Josy's shrill treble tones were singularly welcome to her ears.

" I say, *what!* The Hidden Ways; you've found them? " panted Sally eagerly.

" The gipsies have. It was *them* I found. They've got a camp there." Josy poured out the tale with sparkling eyes. " The woman's nice; she'll let us see their tent. She wanted to tell my fortune, but I asked her to do that instead."

" Will she? Where is she? " Sally was still panting with eagerness and haste. She turned eager, excited eyes to where the wreath of white smoke curled.

As though in answer there came a rustling in the bushes—an excited rustling. The gipsy woman, slightly breathless too, was back again. Her gaze, bright and eager, was fixed upon the pair.

" 'Tis under the tan gentle rawnees, that

the poor Romany folk live," she said in a half whine. " Sure, those who come from the great school will be too proud to visit the camp."

" Too proud. We're not," returned Sally quickly. " We'd love it. I say, you *are* clever : —to find the Hidden Ways, I mean. And clever in other ways, too. How did you know that we come from the school ? "

" The poor Romany folk have need of their wits to win them a living," returned the gipsy woman. " Ah, and we could tell ye greater mysteries than those there." She held back the bushes to let the girls pass.

It was a strange, really a wonderful site for a camp. As hidden as ever were the homes of any of the wild things of the Downs was this Romany camping-place. As the bushes parted, they displayed a little track—scarcely more than a rabbit-run it looked. The girls had to crouch and crawl as they followed their guide, while, but for her help, they would have been blinded by the rough branches which were ready to swing back in their faces at every yard of head- way that they made. But presently the track seemed to open wider, and they found them- selves creeping down to a wider pathway—the old sunken road. The Hidden Ways felt cool and fresh after the glare of the sun on the chalky Downs, and owing to the thick bushes which hid the place, it seemed dark, too; at first, as dark as midnight. But as they stood there, able to stand upright at last, the girls gradually became accustomed to the change; darkness, which had seemed pitchy at first to their unaccustomed eyes, grew twilighty instead. They were able to distinguish objects, and to realize that they were not alone.

Close to them was the tent, from a hole in top of which the coil of smoke had escaped; round them were strewn gipsy possessions in pell-mell. There was a general air of bustle, too, as though the camp had not been pitched there long. Children peered at them from the tent; a dog barked and was quietened again by the angry sound of his master's voice. "Oh, the precious!" cooed Josy, suddenly finding her short skirts gripped by the sticky fingers of a brown gipsy-baby, who lay kicking in an ancient box-cradle.

"I say, how absolutely ripping," declared Sally, addressing their guide.

But the said guide was gone again, and from inside the tent outside which the girls were still standing there came a torrent of un-intelligible talk. It wasn't English, that was certain. It must be the gipsy language, the girls decided, standing still.

Were they going to be shown the interior

of the tent ? They were. But the manner of
their entrance was to prove amazing. Back
through the flap of canvas which served as
tent door peered again the gipsy woman, beckon-
ing them to enter. " Will the rawnees enter
the poor Romany dwelling ? Will ye step under
the tan ? 'Tis just my husband is within,
gentle rawnees, a Romany chye of true blood.
And it's sure with us, yes, that he holds a
letter for one of ye. Look ! "

" A letter ! " repeated Josy, staring.

" A letter ! However could he ? " Sally
stared. " Which of us, eh ? "

" 'Tis truth she's telling you. 'Tis a letter,
writ and signed, sure." They were inside the
gloomy tent now. " Writ and signed by ' Sara
Heath.' " The voice of the man who had
stilled the dog came again from the gloom,
and the girls started. Not only at the extraordinary interruption, but also, as they grew
used to the dimness, at the meaning expression
of the gipsy man's voice. He stood there, in
the tent, eyeing them. His face was not
unfriendly, but it was craftier than that of
the woman. " 'Tis here, gentle rawnees ; 'tis
no falsehood she's told ye. We Romany folk
know a many things that's hid to the rest,
without being good scholards like gentle rawnees
of the great school. 'Tis secret what we know ;

and it is a letter, sure, that we hold—to change, right willing, for the matter of a silver piece."

There was a quick movement of his hand. There and then before the astonished gaze of the girls he held up—a letter, certainly, as he had said ; and just as certainly it was *the* letter which a week ago now the pair of them had dispatched, tied to the wing of the carrier pigeon, down at the " Smuggler's Tea-Cosy," about two miles away across the Down.

" *But—*" Sally voiced her surprise first. She drew herself up, and took a step forward. " That's mine, not yours. Give it to me at once, please."

" Not so fast, gentle rawnee." The man stood still, and the woman stepped between Sally and the letter, talking quickly in a whining voice. " Sure we mean no harm to ye, gentle rawnee. 'Tis having the letter you shall be, yes ; himself wouldn't harm a hair of ye. All we ask is the gift of a silver piece, and the letter is yer own again."

" I haven't got any money," cried Sally angrily. " And the letter's my own."

Josy said nothing. She was still holding tightly to the gipsy baby's sticky fist, and staring at this most extraordinary turn that events had taken.

" Give it back to me," called Sally, " or I'll

tell the police. I never heard of such a thing. Stealing my letter." She took a resolute step forward.

But she certainly was no match for the gipsies, and at the sound of the hectoring tone in her voice the man's tone changed. His voice, too, sounded bullying and insolent. " Stealing, is it ? Ye'll not get back yer letter, my rawnee, for all the police in the country-side. Sure, they knows us Romanies well as honest travelling folk."

" And sure ye'll be the lucky rawnee if ye get yer secret back safe, and all for the gift of a bit of silver money now," put in the gipsy woman ingratiatingly.

" There's some who'll pay for it anyways, I reckon," went on the man, stuffing the envelope into his pocket.

" Pay. Who do you mean ? " inquired Sally.

" The queen rawnee down at the great school ; sure, the one with the silver hair, 'tis she will pay the Romany folk a good price." The man's tone was threatening.

" You mean Miss Dean ? Oh, you wouldn't be such a sneak ? Why, it's mine. It's not yours at all," burst out Sally. But already her voice sounded entreating rather than intimidating. She couldn't face this last idea. " Do you see what he means ? " She turned to Josy.

" He'd take it to school. And Miss Dean would get it, and the story would be everywhere. Perry's never had the letter at all. Oh, Josy, have you any money ? "

Josy shook her head. " I could run over the ridge and fetch Miss Gill," suggested she.

" Fetch Miss *Gill !* Why, that's worse than anything," stamped Sally. " No, there's only one thing to be done." She turned to the gipsies. " Give me the letter, then, and you'll be paid for it," said she, " just as soon as I can bring the money to you. Yes, I'll pay for it after all."

But the gipsy man laughed an unbelieving laugh, and the woman began to whine again. " Sure, rawnee, we Romany folks must look to ourselves. 'Tis little we earns. Sure, we'll hand over the letter, sure, when you bring the silver, sure. Five shillings, rawnee, five silver shillings for luck, will buy it. And till then, why, 'tis safe as the sun in the sky with the Romany folk."

" Oh dear." Sally was panting. " Look here, then, Josy, we'd better go quickly. We may just have time. Oh, bother." To-gether they turned, Josy bending down to kiss the gipsy baby good-bye, and retraced their steps through the bushes. It was not until they had reached the blinding glare of the

Downs again and had left the shadows of the
Hidden Ways that they realized the existence
of the outer world at all.

But then they realized it very fully indeed.
As they crossed the second ridge, hastening
and hurrying and speechless in their speed, suddenly the noise of voices sounded close at
hand. Miss Gill and her returning troop of
junior maidens came hot-foot over the Down.

" *Josy !* " It was Miss Gill's voice. " Where
have you been ? And, can it be *you*, Sara
Heath ? Will you kindly, both of you, explain
yourselves at once ? "

CHAPTER XIV

JOSY MAKES A PLAN

" IT'S absolutely awful. I simply don't know what to do," said Sally. " At any minute, since we never went back with the money, he might take it to Miss Dean." She and Josy were walking together to church.

" I suppose," began Josy for the third time, " you wouldn't just go to Miss Dean yourself, would you, Sally ? "

But she pulled herself up before she had finished the sentence. At the first time of asking the question her companion had literally flown at her.

" If you're such a baby as all that, Josy, then what *do* you understand ? Why, if I did that, I'd have to explain, wouldn't I ? And Miss Dean would know just as plainly as though the gipsies had told her. And she might very likely decide to find out what the secret was."

" Miss Dean's most awfully understanding,

you know," Josy had said with a little shake in her voice.

For Miss Dean had been "most awfully understanding" last night, when Josy, to her terrible dismay, found herself sent before the Head "for a wilful and flagrant violation of understood rules." Those were the words that Miss Gill had used in connection with the afternoon's escapade. Her eyes had flashed, too, and had seemed to pierce Josy through and through.

" Was *this* what you were planning when you went in to speak to Sally before the walk ? " inquired the walk-mistress.

" I think so," said Josy, trying to be truthful.

" And you told me you were saying good-bye. *Well !* " Miss Gill's voice was expressive. " And you slipped away from us, knowingly, to meet Sally ? "

" Ye-es." Josy nodded sadly.

Then had followed the dreadful phrase of long and difficult words which had appeared in Miss Gill's very fair mind to sum up Josy's conduct. " Miss Dean herself will see you about this."

Josy's heart swelled until it almost burst. She couldn't even answer to Sally's congratulatory remarks on the way home. " You're a little sport, Josy, not to tell. Well, anyway, we're safe as to the gipsies. The girls never twigged where we came out. Miss Gill doesn't guess. Only *how* are we to get the money to them now ? "

" Let's tell them all *everything !* " Josy wanted to say. It would have made things so beautifully easy, and all so right again. But somehow, with Sally, things didn't go like that. Josy had to bottle everything up in her unhappy small heart and wait.

But Miss Dean had been understanding, as the little straight-backed girl with the downcast features who had stood before her last night had realized.

" Josy, I did not expect this." The Head's voice had been gentle. " You have never been sent to me like this before."

A dreadful sigh from Josy.

" Did you really break the walk-rules, *knowing* that you were breaking them ? "

" I think so, Miss Dean," whispered Josy.

" And was it your own fault that you did so ? " The Head's voice was level and slow.

" Oh *yes*, Miss Dean." The answer came quickly. Josy looked up eagerly for the first time, for fear Sally should be blamed too much.

" Josy, you won't forget that girls who have been at Beech Trees for some time—even though they are still quite small girls—have a special duty to the new ones who come ?   Do you know what that duty is ? "

" To be kind to them," volunteered Josy.

" That is part of it.   But to help them to play the game, you know, all round.   By keeping the rules, whether written-down rules or not-written-down rules, just because *we* make Beech Trees, every one of us, by our conduct here."

" Yes, Miss Dean."

There had been no mention of Sally.   But Miss Dean understood.   It was the meaning of her last remark that made Josy summon up courage just before the little church was reached.   " Sally, I say—yes, I know it's dreadful about the gipsies having the letter— but won't you tell Miss Dean ?   About the letter and everything.   Secrets are so—hateful."   Then came a quiver in Josy's voice. " Then we could start clear, and keep the rules, and play the game for Beech Trees."   It had taken all Josy's resolution to bring out the words.   She hadn't had a chance to speak to Sally before since the Head's words, for Sally was doomed to yet another fortnight's slumber in the San. owing to her breach of parole. Josy had decided that she would ask Sally as they went to church about keeping the rules

and playing the game. Quivering with shyness, she had done so.

Sally turned, and her next words stung like
a lash. She was feeling unhappy; she was
lonely; instead of standing on a pedestal at
school, she had found herself in very different
case. Her only comfort had been the loyal
Josy, and now Sally turned.

"Look here, Josy, *tell*, is it? You'd get me
into fresh bothers and not care, would you?
Well! and when you come to think of it it
was you yourself who tied the letter on to that
pigeon! I never thought of doing it—I never
would have! So the gipsies, who plainly
stole the pigeon on its way home, and probably
ate it, would never have got the letter at all
but for *you!*"

This was the unkindest cut of all. As the
cavalcade turned in through the lich-gate
Sally repented bitterly that she had let her
temper get the better of her. *What* a beast
she'd been to say it, or think it! What a beast!
For Josy had been a sport. She——

"Sorry, Josy," she whispered.

But Josy, with her head held high and her
cheeks very white, said nothing.

"Josy! I say, kid, cheer up. I never
really meant it. Don't worry."

"But it's true." A little sob broke from

Josy. " And I never thought. I did do it. It *was* my fault, and I never thought of it like that."

" Straight in, girls. Take your places," came Miss Heriot's quiet voice from behind.

Up the aisle went the Beech Trees girls in single file to their usual seats.

Sally's place was just behind Josy's own, and through the service Sally found herself, for a wonder, watching the little set white face ahead round the pillar and wondering, instead of making up plans throughout the sermon, as she had intended to do, for recovering the letter from the camp, if she had made Josy feel unhappy. Josy really was a little brick. No other kid would have been so sporty. Sally was fond of Josy, and she wished she'd had time before church was reached to make the kid understand that she really hadn't meant what she'd said. That she'd only blurted it out in a temper, and had hated herself for saying the words as soon as they were uttered. Well, they would be walking home together, and she would put things right—so Sally told herself—and she would be extra decent to Josy to make up. Perhaps there *was* something in what the kid said, thought Sally, in the quiet, old-time fragrance of the little church. Perhaps there was something to be said for keeping rules if once one could only start clear. But that wretched letter! Her meditation came to an end with the sudden rising of the congregation for the last hymn.

"Hullo, kid," said she genially as she and Josy re-met in the porch. "I've been thinking——"

"And I've been thinking too." Josy spoke in a chirp which sounded rather trembly. "And Sally, I *did*—I mean I *didn't* play the game. And I've been at school longer than you, and we're Beech Trees; so I've *got* to help you get the letter back, but after that I've got an idea." Josy stared in front of her.

"Well?" Even Sally was amazed.

"I've thought, and we'll get the letter back at riding," said Josy in little quick pants. "We could. Rhona's on the guiding-rein, and Mr. Dixon would have to stay with her, and she can't canter. Mary and Lesley are the only other two this term, and they're not so good as us—you and me. So we'll be together behind. Last week, when you rode they gave you Taffy, and he loves the Downs. Well, I'm sure to have Flora, and she's game, I know. We'll head them both off." Josy stopped. She had been speaking almost feverishly.

"Josy!" began Sally, staring.

" We'll head them off when Mr. Dixon isn't very noticing," said Josy, " and race. Perhaps he'll be cross afterwards, but we'll have done it, you see. We'll canter up to the camp, and we'll hand in the money and get the letter. Perhaps Mr. Dixon won't mind. And you can put the letter into your habit pocket—" Josy's voice broke.

" Josy," said Sally, all admiration, " you're a brick, and I'm jolly sorry I said that about the pigeons. It wasn't really your fault."

" But it was—honest Injun, it was," said Josy drearily. " So, don't you see, *that's* why I've thought out this plan. We'll do it, Sally, and then "—Josy stopped again—" then, Sally, oh, let's keep rules for ever and ever and ever. It's so much more comfortable," finished up Josy, with her blue eyes full of tears. " For we *are* Beech Trees, you see."

CHAPTER XV

THE RUNAWAY CANTER

"NOW keep together, young ladies." Old Mr. Dixon, the riding-master, was speaking in his clippy tones. "Miss Rhona, don't hold yourself all stiff now. Keep your seat, yes ; but easy does it. Be at one with your mount, miss. Watch Miss Josy there. Now, Miss Lesley, please." The riding lesson began.

Behind the others rode Josy and Sally. Rhona, a beginner, was at the master's side, on the guiding-rein, as Josy had said. Lesley and Mary were on his right, already receiving instructions as to the correct way of holding their reins. The cavalcade went in stately fashion down the Beech Trees drive.

Josy, sitting erect and centaur-like, was even straighter to-day than usual. Tuesday was her joy-day of the week always, for after home people Josy missed the home pony next. Always on Tuesdays at Beech Trees she woke up extra early with a feeling that something lovely had wakened her. To-day, as she had left dreams behind her, however, there had been a cloudy feeling lowering behind the blue of the day's horizon. What was it? She knew as soon as she had opened her eyes.

Oh yes; it was riding-day, and she would see Flora again, but— Josy sighed as she stretched herself in bed. Oh yes, there was something else. And she had to do it—it was the only way. She had thought it all out in church on Sunday, and she had been sure then that she ought to do it, even though it was difficult to arrange what was right and what was wrong all by one's self. For it must be " all by one's self." On account of Sally Josy simply couldn't ask any one's advice. She only knew, after what Sally had said just outside the church porch, that it was her fault—Josy's own fault—that the gipsies had the letter.

And Miss Dean had said that old girls—even if they were little—must play the game and teach the new ones that way. Well, Josy must somehow set things right, so she had decided, and since it was impossible to ask advice, since Sally certainly wouldn't agree to that, she must, by herself, get the letter back.

" But then," Josy had thought in the quiet

fragrance of the little church, " when I've done that we'll start fair. I won't break any more rules—not for anything; and I'll tell Sally. But first for Beech Trees." Twelve-year-old Josy sighed.

It was strange—or perhaps not so strange—that Sally, just behind her, was beginning to think at that very moment on the still Sunday morning that there was something to be said for rule-keeping, and that if once she could start fair—   That was two days ago now.

" You still game, Josy ? " remarked Sally in an undertone, as they stood on the steps clad in riding-breeches. " I've got that five shillings."

She had spoken in a new tone, almost un-Sally-like and shy. Since the Sunday morning after church, when Josy had burst into tears while at the same moment suggesting an escapade which, for daring, had almost taken Sally's own breath away, the latter had realized the existence of a " something " in Josy of which she had not been conscious before.

Sally considered herself proud, but Josy was proud too. That she had taken in the full significance of Sally's remark as they entered the church and meant to right herself in Sally's eyes was the construction which the elder girl—

who didn't perhaps understand pride in its biggest sense—had put upon Josy's words. But there was more in it, really, than that. Josy's pride in the school itself was touched too—a realization, after Miss Dean's speech of last night, that, as a part of Beech Trees, she had failed in upholding its meaning to the new girl was at the back of the twelve-year-old's mind as she tried to wonder out a way to put things right. The way she had decided upon wasn't what Miss Dean would have suggested, but since " telling " was taboo, it seemed the only way to the well-meaning small muddler groping in the darkness of uncertainty.

For Sally had promised that if the letter was got back she would start fresh and keep rules ; besides which it was " up to " Josy, the child told herself, to get hold of the letter when it was she who had been the cause of its miscarriage. And Josy, although she was unhappy in her daring, meant to carry out the deed all the same. Somehow she felt that she owed it to Sally ; somehow she felt that it was the only way to put things right ; therefore, by some queer method of twelve-year-old reasoning, that she owed it, too, to the school.

She rode beside Sally down the drive with a chin set hard with determination, and with a pink patch on either cheek. She hadn't mentioned the subject again since Sunday. " Game," though ? Of course !

" I'm glad you've brought the money," she said in rather a high little chirp as they passed through the lodge gates. " Of course we're going to do it." She bent down to stroke Flora's glossy neck. Evidently she didn't want to speak on the subject again. But they were through the gates now, and spanking along the hard highroad. In ten minutes or so they would pass the pathway that led to the Down.

" It's a ripping morning," said Sally, feeling light-hearted. " And Taffy's a dear. I was awfully afraid they'd give me some huge horse, not easy to hold. They so often do that in riding-schools. But Taffy's a joy. He knows me already." Sally continued to soliloquize, while her companion rode quietly at her side.

" Not feeling A1 at Lloyd's to-day, Miss Josy, eh ? " inquired little old Mr. Dixon, turning a head. He had noticed an absence of chatter from his favourite pupil. " Flora, now, she's always extra happy, *she* is, on a Toosday, Miss Josy, so the grooms say ! Don't have to give her no extra oats, Miss Josy, for to buck her up, and get her out of the stable. Not on Toosdays." Mr. Dixon laughed. Then he turned his attention to the threesome in his

line, all very much in the learning stages.
" Keep yer elbers in, Miss Lesley. You don't
see no one with no knowledge ride with her
elbers flung out like one of those there windmills up on the Downs. No, no, Miss Rhona,
don't get fussy. Daisy's never shied yet on
the road. If she ever had, you know, we'd not
use her as a mount for a beginner, not we.
But even the best-natured mare don't actually
enjoy the flies."

It was at that instant that the turn to the
Downs came in sight.

" Now," said Josy in a little dry voice.

She turned Flora's head easily, and urged
her suddenly up the turf of the Down.

Sally was after her, with hair flying and eyes
sparkling. This was jolly—an escapade after
Sally's own heart. She was a splendid horse-
woman ; she had never been afraid in her life
of anything at all, at least this was her boast.
For to be afraid of anything, either rows or
adventures, seemed to her a confession of weak-
ness indeed.

" Isn't this delicious ! " panted she, reaching
Josy's side, and cantering along neck to neck
with her companion.

Josy didn't answer.

" I'd give loads to look round, but I'm not
going to," laughed Sally. " I'm sure I heard

him call after us. But he's literally tied to Rhona ; she'd fall off, I do truly believe, without the rein. And the others would squeal if he left them. Of course he may dismount the lot and ride after us ; but then who's to hold the horses if he does ? " Sally gave a ripple of laughter.

Josy didn't speak.

" Oh, Taffy, my angel," continued Sally, " aren't you enjoying this ? Flora is too, Josy. More than you are, I believe. You're not funking, are you ? "

" Along this way. We'll see the smoke in a minute. Then we'll ride straight back, and then, oh, Sally——"

" Eh ? " inquired Sally gaily.

" We'll start even when we've got the letter, and keep rules, and—" began Josy in little pants, just as once more the gipsy woman's head suddenly peered over the bushes which concealed the entrance to the Hidden Ways.

A look of terror and apprehension in her eyes changed to one of relief and delight at the sight of the two girls. " Sure, oh, my gracious, gentle gorgeous rawnees, sure, 'tis terror took me at the sound of the horses' feet. 'Twas myself fearing——"

" Can't wait." Sally was mistress of the ceremonies again now. " We've brought the money. Tell your husband. We couldn't come to the camp till to-day, and we must ride back at once. But give us the letter."

" Sure, himself is——" began the woman with rather a queer look in her eyes, but she stopped and gazed greedily at the coins in Sally's outstretched hand. " Wait now ; will the gentle rawnees wait?" She hastened away.

Flora and Taffy tossed their heads, impatient of flies, and pawed the ground suggestively as the minutes went on. Sally employed the time in chatting to her mount. Josy gazed behind her. No one was in sight. There was no sound at all. The Downs glittered with the full beauty of the summer midday. And yet, in spite of the fact that everything would soon be right again, Josy felt strangely unhappy.

" I wish that woman would hurry up," began Sally for the third time.

As she spoke, up peered the gipsy again, all smiles and apologies. " 'Twas safe as the sun in the sky, rawnees ; and put away careful. Here it is, sure." She handed over the envelope.

The five shillings, too, exchanged owners. The deed was done.

" And now," panted Sally, as they turned

their horses' heads again in the direction of the village, " I'd love to ride all day !

> " Oh, who will o'er the downs with me,
>   Oh, who will with me ride . . ."

sort of way.   But I'm not going to.   Fact is, Josy, you're a little sport, and I promise you——"

It was at that moment, just as they had crossed the smoothest bit of turf, and had gained the last little ridge, that Flora caught her foot in a rabbit-hole and came down, suddenly, unexpectedly, sending her small rider over her head.

" Josy, I say, Josy ! "   Sally reined up and was off at once.   " Josy, are you hurt ? "

But Josy said nothing ; she lay back with her small white face looking up at the deep blue sky.

CHAPTER XVI

JOSY IN THE SAN.

JOSY was dreaming. About bathing in dew-ponds it was. The fairies were bathing, a whole army of fairies. And Josy, in her dream, very badly wanted to bathe too. But something prevented it—something to do with rules, and something to do with Sally. And when she tried to bathe in spite of everything, because she was so hot and thirsty and the dew-pond looked so blue and cool, why, some one (a Down gnome, of course) seized her left ankle and held it tight as in a vice of iron, hurting her terribly.

> " Bathing in a dew-pond
> Is the greatest fun . . ."

Josy had begun to sing, but she couldn't go on. She woke up with a cry instead.

" *Oh ! oh !* please, I never truly wanted to break the rules," cried out Josy.

But the Down gnomes weren't there, though

the pain in her ankle remained. Matron was beside her instead.

"Lie down now," said Matron, in a voice which, even though it was stern, was kind too. "And you'll not need to think about breaking rules again for a while, I guess."

Josy did as she was told. It was the easiest thing to do ; and besides, she would never have thought of doing anything else. And dreams came, more dreams, and in all of them figured Sally instead of Down fairies now, and in all of them figured the pain.

"Hullo, Matron," she said at last, waking up and feeling really and properly awake at last, "would you mind telling me why I'm in bed?"

Matron was nothing loath. In her opinion Josy, so soon as she had swallowed a plate of broth, was quite ready to know. "It's just what you deserve, more or less, Josy," said Matron, who was almost as good at lecturing as at nursing. "Your ankle—well, the doctor gave you something and put it right straight-away. You didn't feel it a mite while he did it. Mr Dixon brought you home. He sent the girls on ahead, and gardener held the horses. Mr. Dixon went over the Down when Sally called him."

There was a very ominous sound in Matron's tone at the mention of Sally's name. Josy couldn't have helped noticing it, even if she hadn't been, as she was, listening with every part of her. It was all coming back to her now.

" Oh, Matron." She tried to sit up. " Stop. It wasn't Sally's fault."

" That's for Miss Dean to decide, I rather think," began Matron. " And you lie down. You won't catch me thinking that *you* led that harum-scarum and *worse* than harum-scarum wild-goose chase—" But at the sight of Josy's wide eyes even Matron, the disciplinarian, changed her tone. " What ? You're not crying with the pain now, Josy ? "

" I'm—*not* crying," sobbed Josy. " But, Matron, it was—I mean it wasn't—it wasn't Sally's fault, and it *was* mine. Oh, all of it— every scrap. And how could Miss Dean know—" Josy put both her sunburned fists into her blue eyes.

" I tell *you* what, tears will hurt your ankle," remarked Matron. " And if it's Miss Dean you want to see, she's on her way up to see you at this minute. Now, will you stop crying, Josy, like a good girl, or will I ask her to go down again ? "

Josy made a tremendous effort, and consequently in two minutes the headmistress herself was duly ushered into the room.

" Oh, Miss Dean—" Josy, flushed and feverish, for the first time in her life forgot her awe of the headmistress ; the pain in her ankle was almost forgotten too—" it *wasn't* Sally's fault."

" Fault, my dear ? " The headmistress sat down by Josy's bed. One cool hand was laid on Josy's hot little paw. " Don't think about ' faults ' just now."

" But I must ; you see, it's mine. I mean— perhaps Sally will get into another ' row.' And she doesn't deserve it. Not this one ; it's mine. And she's not going to break any more rules again for Beech Trees. And this would spoil it so if—" Josy's tears grew a little less. There was something so quiet and understanding and sufficient somehow about the head- mistress's presence.

" Wait, Josy, for a minute, till you have quite stopped crying. Then you may tell me as slowly as you like, if that will make you feel better."

" But I can't tell quite everything." Josy gave a sigh. " But what I want to say, Miss Dean, is, that *I* did it. *I* broke the rules. It wasn't one single scrap Sally's fault this time. Going to the—" Josy stopped herself quickly, for the existence of the camp was Sally's secret, really. " Going on the Down——"

'Tell your story quietly, Josy. There is
no need to hurry and hurt yourself." Miss
Dean's voice was level and kind. "I have
not spoken to Sally on the subject yet."

"Oh, then"—Josy drew a gasp of relief—
"it's not too late. Miss Dean, it's this way.
I said to Sally, truly, I did, 'Let's run away
over the Down. From Mr. Dixon.' And
Sally said, '*Oh!*' like that. So, you see, she
didn't think of it, did she?" Josy stopped.

"Go on, my dear," said the headmistress.

"Well, then, we did it. She came too,
and we did it." Josy stopped. "And as we
came back Flora stumbled." Josy gave a
little shiver.

"And that is all you want to tell me, Josy?"

"There is more; but, truly, Miss Dean,
there's no breaking rules about the rest of it
now. And it *was* me, Miss Dean, who arranged
about the runaway canter. And Sally's never
going to break any more rules now that——"

There was plainly something more behind.
But this, equally plainly, was not the time to
worry the invalid in the matter. Miss Dean
stood up.

"Miss Dean, you do believe me? It was
my fault. I ought to have all the 'row' and
the punishment, not Sally."

"Josy, my child, your part of the 'row,' as

you call it, has been administered already, I think. Your ankle will take time to mend and give you some pain, I am afraid. As for Sally, you may trust me. I promise you that she shall get no punishment nor scolding that she does not deserve, and I promise you that everything you have told me I shall remember in dealing with her." Miss Dean's hand smoothed Josy's wet hair from her forehead. " So now, will you sleep ? "

Josy was asleep again almost before the headmistress had left the room—dreaming of Beech Trees instead of dew-ponds, and of Miss Dean and Matron. But in these dreams, too, Sally moved all the time as the central figure.

Sally, meanwhile, downstairs, was feeling horribly unhappy. At the first sight of Josy stretched out on the Down turf she had gathered all her wits together nimbly enough and had acted sanely and sensibly. She had raised Josy's head a little to a more comfortable position, and had quietened the unhappy Flora, who seemed to know that something dreadful was amiss. Then, having tied the reins to a tree near by, she had set off on Taffy's back to fetch help. It was not long in coming. Mr. Dixon, having disposed of the rest of his charges in the manner which Matron had described to Josy up in the San., was already on his way over the Down. Even Sally, who wasn't afraid, in her own opinion, of anything or anybody at all, had felt the look of scorn in the riding-master's eyes as, without a word, he had made haste to Josy's side.

" Not that it's so much my fault as they think," remarked Sally to herself as, on Taffy's back again, she hastened back to Beech Trees at Mr. Dixon's orders to fetch more help. " Still, I don't care. I shan't let on about that, of course. And I'm most horribly, horribly sorry that Josy fell. I do trust it's nothing serious. I know that at polo I've seen heaps of spills that meant nothing at all. Well, of course, I'll take all *this* row ! "

At first, however, up at Beech Trees, no one, in response to her news, seemed to have any time or thought for Sally herself. After she had been asked and had given the assurance that she herself was fit and not injured in any way, she was told, rather sternly certainly, by Miss Heriot, the second mistress, to return to her classes without delay.

" But," Sally said, staring, " I——"

" Miss Dean will see you later, Sara," Miss Heriot had said. " In the meantime, as you no doubt understand, her wish will be to see Josy at once, when she comes in. *Your* part of the matter will wait."

Sally went into class wishing her part of the matter was over. There was a whole day to be got through, however, before any special notice was taken of her at all. A part of the story had got round the school, of course, by means of the excited tongues of Rhona, Lesley, and Mary. Everybody knew, too, that Josy had been thrown, and was up in the San. The girls looked questioningly and curiously at Sally, but no one asked her for information bearing on the case. " Every one seems to take it for granted, of course, that the whole thing was my idea," thought Sally to herself. " Well, let them ; I don't care. But I jolly well wish I could find out how Josy really is."

An inquiry of Miss Davis, who was " taking games," only received the reply, however, that " Miss Dean has issued no bulletin as yet." The prefects might know, of course, as Sally deliberated, but she simply couldn't bring her-self—great as was her anxiety—to ask them. As the afternoon droned on she watched a cricket practice listlessly, and felt as miserable, perhaps, as she had ever felt in her life. Miser-able in rather a new sort of way, too, though she hardly realized that ; miserable with the suspense about how Josy might be faring upstairs. There *were* lots of mere scratches at polo, she remembered, when she'd watched

with Dad ; but there were sometimes real
pukka fiascos too. How *was* Josy ? she kept
asking herself. Well, she'd promised the kid
to keep rules now that the letter was back, and
honestly she would. As she recalled that last
thought Sally realized that Josy all along had
been absolutely sporting. " It's her keenness
on Beech Trees, partly," thought Sally. " Well,
and it's not truly such a rotten place either, if
everybody wasn't so stand-offish. If it hadn't
been for the beginning of things—" Sally
cheered up, and felt in the pocket of her sports
coat for the envelope. Perhaps, after all, she
could start fair now. " I'll tear the letter up,"
thought she, " and get rid of it." She proceeded to tear open the envelope.

It was after she had done so that she suddenly
gasped and stared unbelievingly for a moment
or two, then turned the envelope over and
over and inside out, and still couldn't believe
her eyes. The envelope was empty. There
was no letter there at all.

CHAPTER XVII

SALLY ALL ALONE

" THEN you have nothing that you wish to tell me ? " said Miss Dean.

Sally was standing in the headmistress's room, to which she had been called after prayers that night. She stood there, facing the Head, looking just as stiff and straight now at the end of Miss Dean's speech as she had looked on entering the room.

" Sally, you wish to hear how Josy is ? " had been her greeting.

Sally did, of course, most dreadfully. But she wasn't going to show her feelings. " Yes, please, Miss Dean."

An account followed of the damage to Josy's ankle. " Dr. Bartlette feared it was broken, Sara. But he has practically decided now that it is nothing worse than a very bad wrench. I saw her this afternoon." The headmistress paused. There had been no word of blame for Sally's part in the matter. Sally was waiting for it, but it did not come yet. " I saw Josy this afternoon," went on the Head in a level tone. " She was in considerable pain. But I think I am right in saying that she was thinking less of the pain then than of another matter."

Sally looked up.

" Of a matter in which *you* are concerned, Sara."

" Me ? " Sally's eyes flashed. The kid had told. Well, it was only to be expected. It was horrible to think of Josy in pain. No wonder she hadn't been able to keep the secret in.

" Josy was feverish, but she spoke quite coherently, and meant every word that she said, I am sure." Miss Dean was speaking again. " I have promised her, therefore, that I will remember all that she said while speaking to you."

There was a pause, during which Sally held herself stiff, her head tilted at an independent angle. She was sorry, hideously sorry, for Josy ; she was glad, really glad, that she was in for a rowing herself, as a kind of make-weight. Miss Dean very likely knew everything, she supposed, about the gipsies and the letter. Had Josy told more ? Had she told, also, about the reason why the letter was written ? Well, but *now* there was something else that Josy

didn't know ! Sally fiercely crushed the scraps
of envelope in her pocket with one hand as she
stood there.

"Josy said"—the headmistress's voice broke
in on Sally's thoughts—"that this morning's
escapade was entirely her own planning. That
was what she had to tell me. She gave me to
understand that you, Sara, were even surprised
at the suggestion when she made it—the suggestion that you should ride away over the Down
while in Mr. Dixon's charge. That is what
Josy told me upstairs. Have I made any mistake, or is she right ? "

" Why—yes—in a way she is," blurted out
Sally. She was absolutely dumbfounded with
surprise. Not that she need have been, as she
reminded herself at once. Josy was an utter
little sport ; she wouldn't have told. " But,"
went on Sally, " I'd rather take the ' row,' of
course. I mean, of *course*, I'm bigger, and I—
don't—care."

She hadn't meant the last three words quite
in the way she might have meant them a week
or two back. Miss Dean looked at her keenly.
Perhaps she understood that.

" But that would not be fair, Sara," she said
quietly ; " and we aim at being fair at Beech
Trees. If the blame is Josy's, certainly you
must not bear the brunt."

" But it's not. Not altogether. Not at all,
really. Not—" floundered Sally. She loathed
the empty envelope which she was crushing in
her hand. If it had not been that the gipsies
had cheated her, things would have been so
much simpler. For now she didn't know *where*
she stood ; she didn't know what the gipsies
might not be planning to do next with the
incriminating letter that they held. For one
instant a remembrance of Josy's suggestion that
she should tell Miss Dean everything romped
into her head. Then she thrust it from her. If
she did, then she'd have to explain back and
back, right as far back as the first day. And
tell everything, and the fool she'd made of herself. No, she decided that she could not do
that. " I don't know what sort of a punishment it is," said Sally, " but I'd rather have it
double, of course, if I may, instead of Josy.
Because——"

" Oh no, Sara." Miss Dean was looking
straight at her. " Life cannot be arranged so
easily as that. If we knew that we could utterly
wipe out our misdoings afterwards by under-
going a punishment which would only punish
ourselves, why, how simple things would be !
But life is *not* simple, and we cannot. Other
people's lives are so much wound in with our
own, my dear, that when we fail, they too

must feel the result of our failures. Our sadness is not only our sadness, if they love us, but theirs too, just as their sorrows are our own also. Even though we ' don't care,' to use your own expression, Sally, we grow to learn to care for *their* sake." Miss Dean stopped.

" I don't think I quite understand," said Sally. But there was a little patch of pink growing in each of her cheeks. Something in Miss Dean's words had struck an answering chord somewhere in Sally's heart.

" Perhaps not yet, Sara. But you will, I hope, sooner or later. And meanwhile I have no punishment to offer you for the escapade of to-day. Josy is bearing it, you see, my dear, for both of you upstairs, where her ankle will keep her prisoner for a week or two at least." Miss Dean rose.

" But—" Sally spoke with a jerk.

" You may go, Sara, unless you have anything that you would like to say to me."

Again Sally had the impulse to tell, but she thrust it back. It couldn't do any good, she told herself ; how could it ? If she could have saved Josy from a punishment, she told herself, then things would be different. But just to make a fool of herself by raking up all the episode of the first day——

" No, thank you, Miss Dean."

" You have nothing that you wish to tell me ? Then, will you go ? "

Sally found her night-things returned to her dorm. that night, and was reinstated in her original cubie, owing to the fact that an invalid was now in possession of the San. upstairs. Sheila and the others, noticing the rather sober looks of the returned one, made her welcome. Miss Dean had dealt with her, as they knew, and it was no part of the Beech Trees girls' code to hammer a girl when she was down. No word of blame was uttered against Sally, and in consideration for her supposed feelings Josy's name was hardly mentioned in the dorm. that night at all. " She will be feeling as rotten as any of *you* would feel if you'd broken a rule and broken some one else's ankle into the bargain at the same time by mistake," Sheila had informed Hesther and Dorothy. " So now, if you've got any tact, show it."

Thus adjured by their head, Hesther and Dorothy did their best, and Sally, feeling really grateful for their consideration, dropped back into her own niche in the dorm.—into her own niche in the school also. Downstairs and in classes the girls seemed, one and all, strangely or not strangely, to have adopted Sheila's view.

Sally somehow found herself taboo no longer, and by virtue of her latest escapade. For they were sorry for her now, sorry because they felt that she must be so horribly sorry herself for the part she had played in Josy's mishap. What that exact part was none of them understood ; but each one of them was conscious how she herself would have felt in such case. Sally needed the help of a stalwart friendly arm to give her a lift back now, in the opinion of the school, and though the opinion was unvoiced, it was none the less strong for that. This was no time for ostracism, therefore Sally found herself readmitted without question into the freemasonry of school.

It was a thoroughly lonely time, though, in spite of the well-meaning efforts of the girls, and Sally grew mopier and mopier. She was quite wise enough and clear-headed enough to understand the attitude of the school, and, as a comrade, she missed Josy even more than ever. Not only as companion for walks, but as confidante in her bothers too. For the bother of the letter was weighing on Sally's mind rather heavily. They had cheated her, the gipsies ; they had returned the envelope absolutely empty, with no enclosure, with nothing whatever within. It was an easy trick, of course. If Sally had not been in such haste on the day of

the exchange she would probably have looked
inside to make sure that everything was as it
should be. Could she possibly have lost the
letter on the way back home, she had asked
herself at first. But no, that was impossible ;
for the envelope had been gummed so securely
that she had been forced to tear it open. No,
it was just a try-on, a regular gipsy trick ;
they had got her money by false pretences, and
they meant further trouble Sally felt nearly
sure.

She was quite sure on the matter before the
end of the first month of term. Days had gone
by more or less uneventfully ; classes alter-
nating with games according to Beech Trees
summer term tradition. It was far too hot
that month for rambles on the Down, and
in the intervals of playing tennis sets or taking
part in cricket practices, Beech Trees, to a
maiden, lay prone on the field, fanning themselves with panama hats and chanting, *à la*
King Richard : " An ice ! An ice ! My king-
dom for an ice ! " in helpless unison.

Sally, " used to India," was able to play
tennis on days when other girls had perforce
resorted *pro tem.* to the above-mentioned efforts
after coolness, and it was while searching
solitarily for tennis balls in a patch of undergrowth at the edge of the fence which

divided the school field from a small lane
that the unexpected suddenly and swiftly
occurred.

" Rawnee ! Gracious rawnee ! " A figure
rose from the ditch.

She might have expected it, Sally told herself. It was the gipsies again. It was the
letter, no doubt.

" Rawnee, gentle rawnee, may a poor Romany
have a word with you, rawnee ? " Oh yes, it
was no other than the whining voice of the gipsy
woman whom they had encountered in the
Hidden Ways. " Anything to get rid of her,"
was Sally's first thought, " before the rest of
the girls catch sight."

" Go away, please," she began urgently,
and then suddenly changed her mind. For,
after all, if the woman did mean to hang round
till Sally spoke to her, what had to be got
through might as well be got through quickly.
" Wait there, then," said Sally. " If you sit
there no one will notice you. I'll be back in
ten minutes or less. But only for an instant,
I can't spare more." She flew off to finish her
set with Sheila, before her absence should be
noticed.

" Deuce game ; deuce set," Sheila was
declaiming while she mopped her heated
brow. " Hurry up ; never mind those balls.

We'll only just get through as it is before tea."

Sally lost. She had known she would. Her mind was full, as she played the last deciding games, of the gipsy woman waiting in the lane.

CHAPTER XVIII

THE GIPSIES AGAIN

" WELL ? " said Sally impatiently.

She had got rid of Sheila, who was even now hieing teawards in a flock with the rest as fast as the heat would permit. Sally would be naturally supposed to be searching for lost balls, of course ; and even as she realized the fact she sighed an impatient sigh. For she didn't want to go back to the shuffling methods of the beginning of term. Even though the last few weeks had been dreary without Josy and depressing with a realization that Josy's hurts were in great measure due to herself, yet Sally felt somehow as though she had reached open country after a scramble through rather muddy undergrowth. She had almost forgotten her fear that the gipsies would pursue the letter-tack further when two weeks and more had gone by and nothing had been heard of them again. They had evidently not approached Miss Dean, and Sally herself had caught no glimpse of them. So life had pursued its way almost as evenly, lately, for Sally as for any other Beech Trees girl ; she had begun, really at last, to feel herself a part of Beech Trees, and to be proud of the feeling. " But I'm jolly glad," thought Sally at intervals, " that I didn't go telling Miss Dean the whole tale. Almost I did, about first day and that letter and everything. Josy's right ; that boy Perry is evidently absolutely too chock-full of things to do at his school, just as we are here, really even to think of writing about me to Sybil, and about the awfully assish thing I did. Shows that I was a bit freshery first off to think he would. Still, I'd hate, just as much and more, perhaps, for the girls to know about it *now !* "

There was a different reason for that. Sally was slowly growing friendly with Beech Trees. She had dropped, or was forgetting she had ever assumed, the " look-at-me-and-wonder " attitude of her first appearance, and was truly settling in. The change had come gradually ; no " rows " could have produced it, though probably the last event in which Josy had figured had helped in some indirect way to bring about the change. The girls were growing chummy with Sally now ; she and they were finding things in common ; tennis and cricket were the themes of the day, and Sally found herself growing as enthusiastic as were the rest of her contemporaries. It was "rotten," she declared impatiently to herself, now just when things seemed rather ripping, that the gipsy episode appeared likely to repeat itself.

"Rawnee. Gracious rawnee." The gipsy woman had been seated motionless as the stone upon which she was resting until Sally, still panting, looked over the fence again; but she rose then with an excited gabble of words.

"Look here, I say, you can stow that. What is it? I've not got much time, and I'm due indoors now," broke in Sally impatiently. She wanted to stem this fulsome flattery. What was it that the woman wanted?

"Rawnee, will you tell the poor Romany how fares the gentle little blue-eyed rawnee who holds the singing-bird always safe in her heart?"

"Josy, you mean, who came to the camp that day?" Sally stared. It couldn't be anybody else but Josy whom the gipsy woman meant, for she had hit off exactly in her picturesque Romany phrase the "something" in Josy which made her the lovable and attractive child that she was. Sally hadn't meant till that minute to do anything but shunt off the woman; but if she really had come just to inquire about Josy, she couldn't do that exactly. "You heard that she was thrown that day, of course," said Sally. "But it's weeks ago. She's nearly well now."

"Sure, rawnee, that's truth; we've been a-travelling since. But I heard that the gentle little rawnee, who kissed luck to my baby, and talked sweet and gentle and low to him, I heard tell that she'd been harmed." The gipsy woman's eyes looked really gentle and sad. "Ah, but it's away we've been, we travelling folk, to the fairs, rawnee, round about. Away from camp, and it's only yesterday we's back again." She looked at Sally with a change of expression in her face. Her voice changed too. "Sure, gracious rawnee," began the gipsy whine again, "and ef you'd cross my hand with a silver bit, why, 'tis the word of himself, and a Romany chye of true blood he is, sure, that you'll get the secret letter back this time, and true."

"I tell you what, I wonder you dare to mention it." Sally stood up straight. She wasn't going to be bullied by the woman, she told herself. "You played me a trick over that letter, both of you. And if you think——"

"Sure, rawnee, 'tweren't no trick at all," began the woman guardedly; "no, my rawnee, no. 'Twas not enough, my lucky lady, dear,

as you brought. Just five shilluns for the value
of the letter, lady, you wrote."

"That's rubbish," said Sally angrily. "You
asked for your five shillings yourselves, and
got it."

"Ah, sure, sure." The woman was watching her. "But it's hard times and hard days
for we Romany folk. And you wouldn't be
guessing the troubles, rawnee, what we travelling folks meets with. Ef you'd find five more
silver shilluns, lady, just for luck."

Sally shook her head. To tell the truth she
hadn't got them. Money wasn't specially
needed at Beech Trees for odds and ends, and
Sally had therefore planked down her entire
finances to purchase a coveted new tennis
racquet. She wanted the letter back, of course,
and she didn't want the gipsies to continue
troubling her. All the same there was nothing
to do but stand firm, she decided. The woman
seemed "nice in parts," Sally told herself,
for she had truly looked sorry when she had
asked for news of Josy. It was more than possible that the request for more money was just
in the nature of a try-on. "I'm sorry if you're
hard up," said Sally, standing her ground,
"but I've practically no money at all left.
Here's a sixpence, if you care to have it. I've
really nothing else." She turned to go.

She was surprised at what happened next. From just round the corner suddenly appeared the gipsy man himself. He had been seated there unnoticed, but evidently keenly listening to the conversation, and he now pressed forward, the crafty look in his eyes showing that he had quite taken in the whole state of affairs.

"Sure, then, five shilluns is little enough, lady," he began, "and a rawnee like yourself can spare more. See here, it's true what she's told yer." He held out a paper between finger and thumb. It was the letter, there was no doubt of that.

"You'd better give it to me. It's mine by rights," said Sally, feeling rather frightened, but sticking to her point. "I paid for it, and I've no more money at all."

"Five shilluns more won't hurt nor harm ye, lady," began the man. "And if you'll refuse the poor Romany folk, 'tis to the silver-haired queen lady of the great school that sure 'twill go."

"I jolly well wish you'd taken it to Miss Dean straight away at the beginning," began Sally angrily. Not that she meant it. She spoke without thinking ; but the man glanced up at her suddenly and inquiringly, as though deciding, on account of her remark, on a change of tactics.

" Sure, there's ill-luck in the letter still for ye, and 'tis true ye'll find it out," he returned angrily. " And there's others will pay for what ye're offered cheap. Ay, there's ill-luck in the letter still." He called out the last words in a threatening tone, and turned towards the moor with the woman following.

" Sure, give the baby's duty to the gentle little rawnee, for luck's sake," she muttered in a half-whisper as she followed the man.

But the last words of the gipsy man were those which remained in Sally's memory. As he reached the moor crossing, and as the woman turned from Sally to hurry after him, her husband raised his voice, and called, " Ay, sure, there's others that shall pay. Young gentlemen is more open-handed mayhaps."

" Whatever on earth did he mean ? " asked Sally of herself. " I'm jolly glad to be quit of the pair of them, though the woman is much better than the man." But the encounter had made her feel decidedly shaky. Her knees trembled as she hurried across the lawn, and it was a relief to find herself in the noisy atmosphere of a whole roomful of tea-drinking and chattering girls. After all, the whole affair with the gipsies had only taken a few minutes, and her lateness passed unnoticed. But in spite of that fact, and although the room buzzed round her with animated talk of games and school things generally, the Romany man's last words were still ringing in Sally's mind all that day.

There was ill-luck in the letter still, was there? Pooh! Sally wasn't in the least superstitious, she told herself, and he had only tried to frighten her into stumping up another five shillings. The last remark that he had uttered, however, had been of an entirely different kind. He had suggested that young gentlemen were more open-handed than young ladies. Did he mean—could he mean?—that he intended to go Perry-wards with an offer to sell *him* the letter? Pooh! Sally tried to banish that idea, too, to the limbo of things forgotten. But it would not go. She found herself forced to grapple with the thought. The gipsies were quite likely to have kept in mind, even if they had not copied it down as they might well have done, the name on the envelope which they had returned to Sally. Perry's name had been written there, and the name of his school. "Gipsies can read and write, I suppose," Sally told herself, "after a fashion anyway. I remember somebody saying once at Granny's that they're obliged by law to go to school. Well, they've read the letter, naturally, and they might go to Perry. But what for? Surely

they'd get as good as they asked for if they did !
Oh, they wouldn't ! "

Having thus reduced the idea *ad absurdum*,
she felt able to settle to her home-work. " I'll
tell Josy when she comes down," she told
herself. " No, though, I don't believe I will.
She doesn't know that I never got the letter
back, and as she's had enough bother out of the
affair already, and is about as white-faced as a
kid can be, I rather think—" Sally stopped.
Josy should not know, she decided definitely.
This last part of the gipsy episode should be
Sally's own secret, even after Josy should come
downstairs.

For the first sight of Josy's small white face
upstairs in the San. had awakened in Sally the
feeling that she had felt once or twice at first
for her smaller friend—a feeling akin to her
love of Puck, the pony at home. Every time
she had visited Josy on the broad shaded balcony where the convalescent spent her days,
that same feeling had stirred in her again, until
it had somehow become a permanent part of
the elder girl's affection. No, Sally decided
that Josy should not be told that the letter
had never been delivered, and that the runaway canter over the Down had not, in spite
of its daring, wrought the result expected.
There was no need for her to know that the

gipsies had figured on the scene again lately,
nor that the letter was still in their possession.
" But I wonder, I do, what he jolly well meant
by that last remark," thought Sally. " If he
meant Perry——"

She fell asleep that night still wondering.

CHAPTER XIX

MATRON'S PICNIC

HALF-TERM! Ripping weather for it too—blue and clear and cloudless. One part at least of the school was gone, of course, to spend the long exeat week-end with friends and relations, but the smaller part remained. A wildly exuberant part it was too; by no means cast down and dispirited because Fate had decreed that a termly holiday spent at Beech Trees was to be their lot.

Half-term at Beech Trees was " topping," to quote the victims. " No rules, practically every prefect away, tennis courts free—*and* Matron's picnic ! " Enthusiasts summed up the joys ahead while Sally listened.

For Sally was to remain at Beech Trees owing to an enforced absence from home of her grandmother ; and though at first she had felt inclined to bemoan her lot, yet the sight of the hardly less wildly enthusiastic damsels left behind, after wildly enthusiastic week-

enders had disappeared stationwards in the
school brakes, had certainly served to mitigate
her fears of possible boredom. Perhaps half-
term at Beech Trees *would* prove to be topping
after all.

" Matron's picnic ? " inquired she, rather
dubiously.

Matron's picnic was the *crème de la crème*
of the summer week-end, so Sally was informed. Matron, it appeared, though inclined to be unbending and severely autocratic
on every other day of the year, was second to
none as companion and ally on half-term week-
ends. Most of the mistresses, having homes
of their own to which (strange though it
might seem to their adorers) they were as keen
to fly when occasion permitted as were the
girls themselves, had already disappeared into
the unknown, to reappear tanned and travelled-
looking on the following Tuesday morning.
Miss Dean would remain, " of course, for
she'd *never* want to go away," Sally was informed ; " but it's Matron who is *it* at half-
term. And now that Josy's off, and there's
no one, by good luck, ill in the San., she'll be
absolutely free for her picnic, and it will be
utterly scrum."

For Josy was " off " in more than one sense.
Her illness had proved rather more lengthy

than had at first been considered likely. Head-
aches and bad dreams and excited, sparkle-
eyed days had been some of the symptoms
which had resulted, over and beside the badly
strained foot, in consequence of the " throw."
" Slight concussion," had been Dr. Bartlette's
diagnosis. " Keep the child quiet. No dis-
turbing visitors. Plenty of fresh air, of course,
and plenty of rest."

As a result Josy had been granted no girl
visitor at all for a while. Her days had been
spent on a long couch on the San. balcony,
and Matron, who really was " a darling lamb
who sometimes dressed in the most frightful
wolves' clothing to disguise how nice she
really was "—to quote Josy herself—had certainly tended her like the most devoted slave.
Hilary had been selected by Matron as the
first visitor, and all other visitors were ordered
to " come in twos and mind you talk quietly,
please, and to each other more than to Josy.
It's tiring for her to talk much, but it will do
her good to listen and hear all the news."

Thus it was that Sally had never yet visited
Josy alone. She had taken tea with Josy, by
the latter's earnest invitation, on several occasions, but always with either Matron or another
girl in attendance. Two weeks ago Josy had
been readmitted to the school grounds, but

there was always an attentive medley of juniors surrounding her in school off-hours. Last week Josy, one step nearer to complete recovery, had been permitted to join the junior walks ; but only very, very short walks, in which Sally, by reason of being in the Middle School, had no part. So it had happened (as the best-laid schemes of headmistresses and matrons *do* happen) that Sally and Josy had never, since the accident, had five minutes' conversation in solitude together.

However, after the half-term, Josy was to return from home " just as well as ever." Dr. Bartlette had " passed her " for school walks, though games were still taboo, and her own bed in her own dorm. was to receive her again. But Sally was looking forward to Josy's return, somehow, with a kind of queer shyness.

For Sally had changed quite a lot in the few weeks that had passed since Josy's accident on the Down. She was settling in at Beech Trees. She was beginning to be content to be a Beech Trees girl without desiring to flash there like a burning, glaring light at which everybody must stare. She had made lots of acquaintances, too, now among the girls who had come forward in Sally's hour of loneliness, and who, finding that the new girl was " quite a good sort, really, when she drops trying to crow," had stuck to her for the pleasure of her company.

Sally was rather enjoying classes too. She already had singled out several mistresses as being really awfully clever and jolly. She wished, in her heart of hearts, since her zest for games and work was growing with the days, that she had been content to " start " this way. She saw now that she'd been something of an ass to begin with, though none of the girls appeared ever to have thought so. " They probably didn't notice me much," thought Sally. " Well, I wish I hadn't made such a fool of myself first day, and I'm jolly glad they don't know of that. The fire-bell was bad enough ! Not that they'd have thought much about the first-day horror, I hardly think, knowing school as I do now. But *since* I wrote that letter, and really made such an idiotic fuss about a little thing—for that's truly what it was, as Josy said at the time—I'd simply loathe the girls I'm getting friendly with now to know that I was so fussy and excited over it ! " Yes, looked at in the truer perspective of things as viewed at Beech Trees, that first-day travelling episode was beginning to appear small and insignificant to Sally.

But yet—queer !—the smaller and more insignificant it appeared, the less Sally wanted

Beech Trees to know how greatly it had worried
and fussed her at the time. "They hate fuss,
and they'd absolutely despise me, or sit on
their heels and yell to hear what a fluster I was
in, and how I wrote that letter, and—yes, how
I bothered Josy—for I did—till she thought
out the pigeon stunt. That's what started it,
and then—" There was so much, and it
had been built from so little; and the very
fact that it had been built from so little was
the reason why Sally still didn't want Beech
Trees to know. "I'm just ordinary here now,
and I want to go on being just ordinary," was
the summing-up of her feelings—very different
feelings from those of a few weeks before, but
understandable all the same. "Of course Josy
knows everything; but she's different."

Josy *was* different; and it was ripping to
think of her coming back, although she wasn't
to know, as Sally was still decided, one word
about the last thing that the gipsies had done.
Yet Josy would be comrade again, cubie mate
once more, and she would always be, small
girl though she was, Sally's chiefest chum of
all by her first choice.

Meanwhile, half-term with all its joys!
Meals in the mistresses' dining-room at small
tables, "like a hotel!" Meals entirely off
school-lines, with Matron, an absolute sport,

urging one and all to take more eggs, or honey, or marmalade, or whatever it might be, as though she had never pressed Gregory powder under their reluctant noses with the same request uttered in sterner tones. Tea in the garden, bed at 9.30, and no rule about talking in bed at all. Tennis before breakfast. " Of course, if we were babies and rotters she could rope us in in a twinkling," remarked Sheila, also one of the left-behinds; " but who *would ?* "

No ; no roping-in was necessary. Time flew on golden wings until the Monday appeared, which was, at one and the same time, the last day of the week-end and the picnic day as well.

" It *is* to be to the Wishing Pool. Matron says we may," came the confirmation, at last, of their wildest hopes.

For the Wishing Pool lay farther afield than most school-walk times could compass, and consequently was a much-coveted expedition. " It takes us ages. We drop over the ridge by the ' Smugglers' Tea-Cosy,' and get right into smugglers' country," somebody told Sally. " The Pool is awfully weird—bottomless, you know, or else filled with ghosts. Anyhow, it's awfully uncanny and eerie, and you can't hear a sound. Your wishes come true, too, if you

wish while you're there. Mine did anyhow;
and other girls say the same. I got the bike
I wanted bang off (of course my birthday *did*
come just about then !) ; and Mary was one
of the winners in a comp. she was in for, and
she'd wished for *that*. Oh yes, we always
wish ; but the main thing is that, if we
go at half-term, you see we have lunch
there ! A whole-day picnic, and then back
to tea at Mary Hinnigan's ' Cosy,' and home
with the owls howling and the spooks hooting,
and Matron enjoying it as much as we do—
every step ! "

This certainly sounded promising, and the
start-off during the morning seemed suggestive
of ripping times ahead.

" We'll go slowly," remarked Matron, emerg-
ing. " After all, till to-morrow, we've got all
the time there is to do what we like with !
Now, girls, share round the baskets, and we'll
drop over the ridge to the ' Cosy ' as we go, and
order our tea to be ready as we come back.
We'll be able for a bottle or two of lemonade
on the way, I rather think, and we can pick
it up there as we go." Matron gazed at the
sky. " And probably Mary's strawberries aren't
over."

They started.

Over the Down, easily and care-free, for

two miles at least, before the " Smugglers'
Tea-Cosy " was sighted below.

" Mary will be looking out for us. She
knows it's half-term," suggested some one.
" Wonder she's not waving."

" Probably she's hastily uncorking lemonade
bottles," suggested some one, " with a vision
of our dry throats."

" Or picking strawberries," suggested some
one else.

" I trust *and* hope," remarked Matron, the
picnic organizer, " that she's not away from
home ! "

Mary was *not* away. But things were worse
than that. As the girls drew near to the little
cottage Mary herself, apparently hastily drying
her eyes on an apron, hastened to meet them.

" Oh, wirra, wirra ! " Her Irish eyes were
red, and her Irish tongue broke out in lamenta-
tions instead of greetings. " Oh, wirra, *wirra !*
Sure we've lost the luck ! "

CHAPTER XX

COUNTERFEIT NOTES

THE girls who had spent their holiday at home, on re-arriving that night from the station, primed with tales of exciting adventures, found their own yarns capped by the story told by the Beech Treesites who had stayed behind. Short was the tale, certainly, but as startling as it was short.

"*What!*" The word seemed to fly from the amazed throats of every returned one with the sound of a bullet ping. "*What!* Are you sure?" Eyes opened widely with horror.

"Sure!" everybody was informed in hushed accents. "Ab-so-*lute*-ly! Wish we weren't. We were on our way to Wishing Pool. Not that we ever got there, of course, for Matron simply couldn't leave Mary for ages. She was in such a state, and do you wonder? Yes; the police were there this very morning. Raided the 'Cosy.' Isn't it dreadful?"

" Dreadful's not the word. It's hideous. It's unthinkable. *Mary!* Why, she's as honest as we are ! "

" Of course. Not that it's Mary they suspect, you know. It's Hinnigan, her husband, that they've taken. On suspicion only, of course. Let's jolly well hope they'll hurry up and release him with apologies. But they say that they—the police, you know—have been suspicious for some time. That counterfeit notes have been found in other people's hands, and that there were a number at the ' Cosy.' "

" Counterfeit notes ! D'you mean to say that they think Joe Hinnigan *made* them ? "

" Ask me another. Nobody could get a word out of Mary. She was dissolved in tears. It had only just happened an hour or so before we came. Matron told us, after a bit, that we'd better all bunk on to the Down and leave her alone with Mary, which we did. Well then, after an hour or so, Matron came along and told us pretty well as much as she knew."

" Well ? "

Girls stood in groups in the garden at Beech Trees, still hatted and booted, still carrying suit-cases ; in the cloakroom they forgot everything save the misfortune that had fallen —by mistake, of that they felt sure—on the good-natured owners of the " Tea-Cosy." It was just as well that there were no rules till next day, and that every one was free still to do as they listed ; for Beech Trees would have found it difficult indeed to switch off their thoughts at this juncture to any other subject.

" Mary—poor Mary ! And Joe—why, he's a brick ! He was gardener at The Beeches boys' school. That was how he met Mary —parlour-maid there. Why, how could it be ? "

" That's what we said to Matron when she came back from comforting Mary. She told her—Mary had, you know—the whole tale as soon as we were gone. Mary says there were notes in a hidey-hole in the cottage ; but that Joe had sold a horse at the fair at Ockstead last week for a good sum, and had meant to buy another next week at Buxfield horse fair. He'd hidden the notes, and when the police came along and said they'd a warrant to search the house, why, Joe didn't show the notes and was silly over it, Mary said. Never having had so much money in his possession before, he'd hidden it away, and he pretended a bit about it. Anyhow the police came upon the notes, and they were all counterfeit ones, and Joe was walked off. The police were kind enough to Mary and told her that Joe

would get off, sure ; and let's hope he will,"
finished up the narrators.

" He will. Oh, he must, of course."

" Well, Matron said there might be com-
plications. She rather hummed and hawed,
as though Mary'd told her more than she
passed on to us. She said that the police
would never have come down like that on the
' Cosy ' unless they'd got some good reason.
She said the police must have received information."

" Counterfeit notes ! As though poor old
Joe could make them ! "

" It's not that they think he did *that*, juggins !
Matron says that for a month or more the banks
and the police have been trying to find clues,
because notes have been circulated in the
county. Somewhere or other somebody is
making them, and some one else is passing them
round the countryside. That's what the bank
manager told Matron, she said, one day this
term. Well, she says, too, that the police
probably think that Joe's been helping some
one to pass them, you see, and getting a share
of the profits. That's all."

" ' All ! ' Why, then, he'd be accessory
after the fact all right. It would mean he'd
been in league with the note-maker gang whoever they are."

" It mightn't. He might not understand, or something like that."

" Well, anyhow and anyway, it's perfectly frightful. *What* a mid-term holiday for them, poor things ; for, of course, they're innocent," was the general summing-up of the case.

But little supper was eaten that night, and stories of home-doings sank back into insignificance. Mary held a warm corner in the heart of every Beech Treesite by virtue of her kindly ways. In a sense she seemed a dependent of the school, relying in some measure, as she did, for custom from the Beech Trees girls. Talk that night up in the dorms., where the no-talk-in-bed rule was still in abeyance till to-morrow, centred entirely round the occupants of the " Smugglers' Tea-Cosy."

" I wouldn't like to be Mary there to-night, all alone with the owls and the spooks."

" Well, she's not alone, as it happens. Matron saw to that. Sent one of the maids down to the village to tell Mary's mother and dispatch her off to look after Mary. They'll probably shut up the ' Cosy,' I should think."

" It's almost as though the cottage was unlucky. Perhaps it *is* haunted like they say."

" Idjut ! "

But as the hour grew nearer midnight ghost tales seemed impossible to keep out of the conversation. "The Tea-Cosy" stood, as every one knew, on the very border of smugglers' country, and it was in and out of the old smugglers' tales that the ghosts came and went.

"The smugglers invented them. The ghosts are all bunkum, of course," Sheila informed her dorm.

"So *you* say, safe in this dorm., but the villagers don't. There's not one of them would cross the churchyard after dark along that side where the Haunted Smugglers' Tomb lies. There used to be a path there, but there's no path now, for the woman in the post office told me when I was buying a post-card of it. It's all grown over, for no one ever dares to walk that way. And then there's the Wishing Pool. Sally, you've missed seeing that, since your picnic fizzled out. But it's awfully eerie."

"Um," said Sally, "*I* wouldn't mind sleeping in the 'Tea-Cosy' alone, or crossing the churchyard by the Haunted Tomb!"

For, frankly, she didn't believe one mite in ghosts or ghost tales; she had had too many Indian magic tricks explained down to humdrum common sense by a mathematical father to believe very much in superstitions. It was quite interesting, though, to lie back in bed and listen to the yarns which hurtled through the dorm., and it was extra ripping because Josy, as of yore, was in the next cubie again, listening too.   For Josy had returned to Beech Trees chirpy and cheery as ever, and feeling as game and full of beans as could be wished. She, too, had lain listening silently to the stories, but now she lifted her voice.

" *I* would, though.   I mean, I wouldn't like at all to sleep in the 'Cosy' alone.   I know exactly how Mary feels, for I've always hated ghosts.   And even if it's stupid, I'm glad she's got her mother."

" Josy ! "

" Well, I am.   I don't know why I mind ghosts, but I do.   Not that I believe in them, not a scrap, really.   But I'd have to try most frightfully not to race if I had to pass the Haunted Tomb.   At the Wishing Pool, too, I think it's horrid : all gruey and Grimm's fairy-tale-ish.   And it's true, so there.   You needn't laugh at Mary, for other people besides her feel the same."

It had taken a certain amount of bravery in Josy to make this declaration, as was evident by the gasp with which she completed her narrative.

" Right-o, Josy," returned Sheila.   " We probably understand Mary's feelings too.   After all, everybody's made about the same, with courage or not courage thrown in to mark the difference. Nobody's ever earned the hundred pounds yet, by the way, I rather believe, which is supposed to be offered to the hero who'll spend the night alone with Madame Tussaud's Chamber of Horrors, and *they're* only wax-works, and not ghosts!" Everybody laughed and turned over to slumber.

But in spite of having every intention of following the example of the rest Sally found it difficult to drop off. The day had been an exciting one, and she hadn't realized until Josy was actually returned how glad she was to have the child back once more. Just the same as ever she seemed, too, not changed a whit. Though they had had no time alone with each other, yet Sally knew that quite well. But she herself *had* changed; she realized that quite clearly with the return of Josy to school. She felt that, somehow, the protecting element in her affection towards the child had grown and grown until it was far bigger than she had known it could be.

For Josy, Sally was beginning to realize, was wrought of feelings as fine as was her willpower strong. She was not one of those children who have never known fear; she was timid, and knew it, and could understand Mary Hinnigan's fears and frights, just as she had understood Sally's own fusses and flusters on the first day. And yet, small as she was, she was the bravest kid, Sally told herself, that she had ever seen. All the braver, perhaps, because her childish bravery was wrought of recognized and conquered fear.

"Of all the girls here, she'd brave spooks soonest, even though she does own to funking them," thought Sally, turning over. "Well, I'm going to let her rest easy over that letter anyway. With any luck I shan't hear from the gipsies again." She was dropping off to sleep, into a muddle of dreams, when suddenly, only half-dozing, she sprang into complete wakefulness again. There were voices speaking in the corridor outside. Sally lay drowsily listening, only half-awake. Who could it be? Well, there were no rules to-night. Oh yes, they were two of the prefects' voices. She could distinguish them—Barbara and Sybil.

"Glad you've got back, Sybil." The head girl's voice was welcoming. "Miss Dean said she'd had a wire and that you mightn't come till to-morrow. Anything wrong?"

"I've got back,"—it was Sybil's tones— "but only just. Knew I'd have to if I could. It's such a horrible example to the rest if a prefect doesn't turn up to time after an exeat. But "—Sybil's voice sounded queer—"I could hardly leave my aunt. She's in an awful state. You know that cousin chum of mine, Dick Perry? Well, of course he was expected home. Didn't come. Most dreadful trouble at his school. Those pigeons, you know, I told you of . . . A letter . . ." The conversation came in scraps, broken up by whispered ends of sentences. Sybil's voice was low too ; but suddenly Sally found herself, almost unconsciously, sitting up and listening with all her ears. Then as the voices died away she pinched herself to make sure that she was really awake.

CHAPTER XXI

SALLY AND SYBIL

SALLY still disliked Sybil. Not personally, perhaps, for there was something sterling and steady about Sybil which must command her respect. But Sybil, in Sally's mind, always seemed, more or less, like a mine which might suddenly explode if one went too near. It was best to keep out of Sybil's beat, Sally had decided. For Sybil was Perry's cousin. Though no word as to Perry had ever passed Sybil's lips in Sally's hearing since that night in the first week of term when the prefect had announced the relationship, yet Sally had never forgotten it.

For Perry was in possession of Sally's secret, and weak and feeble as that secret seemed now in the light of a larger life than that of a few weeks ago, yet how weakly and feebly Sally had figured in that first escapade of hers she now realized, and therefore the circumstances would, she hoped, lie for ever in the oblivion they deserved. On Sybil's duty-days Sally always hastened through her dressing and undressing in the cloakroom, kept rules rigorously, and punctiliously kept out of this particular prefect's way. She desired to be unnoticed by Sybil, just in case ! And, so far, her wish had been granted.

" I must say the new girl Sally in Sheila's dorm. simply gives no trouble at all now," Sybil had announced placidly at a prefects' meeting. " She may have broken rules downstairs, but in the corridor you'd not know—after the fire-bell business, of course—that she is there at all."

But to-night Sally suddenly realized that Sybil must be approached. She'd simply got to go. The gipsies had done their worst, that was certain. If Perry was in a row that had something to do with a letter and with pigeons, then there was no doubt of what Sally must do. She sat up in bed and deliberated, staring into the darkness as she did so. Six weeks ago she wouldn't have done what she was going to do, but now, with Josy sleeping in the cubie beside her, she made up her mind. Partly on account of Josy. If there was going to be trouble about the letter Josy shouldn't know of it. Josy was unaware that the gipsies had given further trouble—well, let her remain so. She herself had had enough to do with the matter. Sally loathed going to beard Sybil in her den, but evidently go she must. It was, she realized, what any Beech Trees girl would do in such a case. And she was Beech Trees. Into a dressing-gown she slipped and out of the dorm. Then she was at Sybil's door.

" Hold ! I say, who's there ? What's up ? " came the reply to her knock. And Sybil opened to her.

The prefect had taken off her hat and thrown her suit-case on to the bed, and cocoa was already steaming on the gas-ring. The room looked cosy and just the same as it had looked on that first night, the last time Sally had visited it. Last time she had been invited, this time she had unwillingly invited herself.

" Sally ! You ! Any one in your dorm. ill ? " Sybil's eyes became business-like at once. Her bothers were thrust aside for the responsibilities that her position demanded.

" No. But I say, Sybil, I wanted to tell you something. You see, I heard—" Sally was stammering.

" You'd better come in, or you'll have every one awake," said Sybil in a business-like tone. She didn't in the least know what Sally wanted, and she had never, perhaps, been more in the mood to be left alone by Sally. One of her own contemporaries would have been wel-

come just now as a confidante, but no one else.
" Yes ? " said Sybil, standing upright. " Here,
put my burberry on over that dressing-gown
if what you've got to say will take long."
She did not offer the midnight visitor a seat.

" Well, it's this," Sally began nervously.
" I heard—" She paused and continued,
" You woke me, as a matter of fact, talking to
Barbara outside our dorm. The rest didn't
waken. Well, it happened that I heard your
cousin's name in what you said."

" My cousin ? Yes ? " Sybil was staring
now, certainly ; she waved her visitor to a seat
on the bed. But Sally preferred to stand up
to the job she had in hand.

" Well, I thought I ought to tell you that—
What I heard you say, you know. Partly because naturally I wasn't meant to hear your
private concerns. But also because—well, it's
not private to me exactly. You see, I think
I'm—mixed up in it."

" *You ?* " stared Sybil. " I say, you're not
dreaming, are you, by any chance ? "

" No, I'm not." Sally was going full tilt
now. " It's only that I heard what you said."

" But how do you know Dick Perry ? " inquired Sybil.

" I don't. At least, hardly at all. I travelled
up in the train with him and his friend."

" Oh, I seem to remember." Sybil passed
a hand over an evidently tired brow. " Just
at the beginning of term, in his first letter, I
think, he said that he and Bob Pollitt had
travelled up with one of our freshers. I hardly
noticed it at the time. Was that you ? "
Sybil seemed hardly to recall the piece of information, so insignificant it was. And it had
loomed so large, so large ! in Sally's mind !
And Perry had mentioned—as she might have
guessed he would not—nothing whatever of
the pickle in which she had found herself on
his own school door. Sally blinked.

" Well ? " It was Sybil's voice again.

" Well, there was something I did. I wrote
to him. Sent a letter by one of his pigeons,
and—when I heard you mention letters and
pigeons and rows——"

" My good Sally ! " Sybil suddenly laughed,
a very tired, rather impatient sort of laugh.
" As though— Seems to me that small matters
loom large in your mind. *You* get him into
a row by any letter you may have written ;
though, of course, it's utterly against rules to
do a thing like that. No, it's a great deal
worse, I'm afraid, than anything *you* could
have helped to bring about." Sybil's voice
changed and the impatient note left it. " Not
that it's not uncommonly good of you to come

along," she said in a heartier tone, " though it's a bit weird of you too. I wish it had been anything so simple. But it isn't. My cousin is in very bad trouble indeed."

" Yes ? " Sally's relief for herself, in spite of Sybil's last statement, couldn't help but be tremendous. She had nerved herself up to the sticking-point, and now she need not be-little herself in Sybil's keen eyes after all.

" Fact is," went on Sybil, " it can't be kept secret long. I hear that the affair down at the ' Cosy ' is all over Beech Trees already. The counterfeit notes, I mean."

" Yes." Sally nodded.

" Well, then, it's got mixed up with The Beeches, where my cousin is at school. That's the long and short of it. Hinnigan, who used to be gardener there, has always been friendly with the boys, and he undertook to manage some pigeon-post affair, it appears, between himself and them. Well, he's been passing counterfeit notes to them—or, at least, that's what the authorities say. And several have been found in Dick's possession."

" *Oh !* " Sally's eyes grew round. Could the gipsies be mixed up with this ?

" Dick Perry was gated for the half-term exeat just at the last, and didn't turn up at home, because he wouldn't explain. My uncle

went down. I stayed with my aunt till he came
back. Dick seems to be holding silent for
Hinnigan's sake; that's what my uncle thinks.
It's the most detestable state of affairs. You
can imagine——"

"*Oh!*" Sally's voice was intense with horror.

"It's awfully good of you to feel so jolly
sympathetic," said Sybil in a nice voice. "Fact
is, I ought not to keep you up telling you.
But you happened to come along and start the
subject just when I was feeling unable to keep
it all in. Well, that's how the matter stands.
So you see"—Sybil smiled a weary smile—
"nothing that you could have done would
have helped him into *this!*"

"But suppose—I mean, it wasn't only a
letter I sent. I mean that the letter *was* sent,
but——" broke in Sally.

"Look here"—Sybil assumed prefecty airs
—"you evidently have been breaking rules,
for we don't dispatch letters to Beeches boys
from here—and certainly not by their pigeons.
And I advise you—mind I shall keep your
words confidential—but I advise you to go
and tell Miss Dean what you've begun to tell
me. *I'm* not the person to come to, but I
advise you——"

Twelve o'clock boomed out from the village
church below.

" You'd better turn in," suggested Sybil in a more comrade-like voice than she had ever used to Sally before. " It's to-morrow, and rules are in force again. But turn over what I've said, though," continued the prefect, " as to telling Miss Dean."

Sybil went back to her own room after escorting Sally to her dorm. " The kid was only half-awake, I believe," thought she ; " not able, anyhow, to put two and two together. Fancy imagining—" Sybil got into bed.

Sally got into bed too, feeling relieved and yet still vaguely uneasy. She had so nearly told. Somehow she wished that she had got the matter off her mind. But Sybil had been so insistent that nothing she could have done could have brought about Perry's trouble, and Sally herself was inclined to agree. " Tell Miss Dean the whole story ! Why, there's no need for that, surely," she told herself ; " and I'd simply loathe and hate to do it now."

CHAPTER XXII

THE OXFORD " WHOLE "

THE school was full of the matter, as might well be expected. Gradually, too, by help of the day-girls, further particulars became known.

" Some of The Beeches boys are in it ! "

" *What ?* "

" In league with Hinnigan—at least, that's the latest rumour, but you know what rumours are. It isn't likely, is it ? But there's even a rumour that some of the boys *made* the notes ! "

" What utter, drivelling rot ! As though—"

" Treasury notes aren't so jolly hard to make, it seems. Just for a joke, perhaps, you know."

" Shut up ! "

But in spite of the fact that mistresses and prefects tried to snub the subject down after a time, there was hardly any wonder that it continued to be the chief topic of conversation. The Beeches lay only five miles by the Down way from Beech Trees. Several of the Beech Trees girls owned brothers and cousins there ; the Beeches caps were generally present at the Beech Trees sports ; and, as return compliment, many of the Beech Trees girls had visited their Beeches relatives for Speech Day. At this moment the Beech Trees girls felt extraordinarily in sympathy with the Beeches boys.

" I jolly well wish we could do something to clear up the mystery," was the burden of many conversations. Plainly a " something " was needed, in the opinion of the Mistresses' Room, to change the topic now.

The " something " arrived in the Oxford examination results. Generally they were good, for Beech Trees worked hard and played hard. But this year the results were voted super-good. No less than five Honours candidates appeared in the lists beside the name of the school, and a whole wealth of distinctions dotted the pages of the exam. lists. Beech Trees was even congratulated by the examination authorities, and Miss Dean proceeded to act upon the congratulations for the good of the school.

" I am very pleased to announce these successes ; and I have decided to announce, too, at the same time, that a whole holiday will be granted to-morrow in honour of the girls who have done so particularly well."

A half had been expected: generally a half followed the announcement of these results. But a whole day! This was unprecedented in the school's annals. The cheers that followed the announcement left no doubt as to the feeling in the minds of the girls. The chatter as they left the Hall was on one subject and one only, and that *not* the mystery of the notes.

"What'll we do, d'ye think? Exeats in twos and threes to the 'Cosy' and the village and round about; that's what happens generally on the Oxford half. But if it's to be a whole day —wheesh!—it's sure to be something special!"

But the prefects were aware, as the rest of the school was not, that the whole holiday had been partly decided upon by the authorities just to change the usual routine of exeat twos and threes. While this counterfeit-note mystery was still unsolved that favourite rendezvous, the 'Cosy,' was forbidden to the girls; the village, too, was forbidden except with special permission. A whole-day picnic further afield was therefore to be the arrangement.

"The Wishing Pool? Oh, let's hope and trust! We didn't get there at mid-term, so perhaps—" The occupants of the dorms., on the night preceding the holiday, forsook the topic that had enthralled them for a fortnight and more for another.

" The mistresses come, and it's topping ! "

" Food goes down in the pony-trap with Dilly-Dally the pony." So on, and so on.

Next day confirmed their hopes : a whole day's picnic to the Wishing Pool it was to be.

Whole-day picnics from Beech Trees to the Wishing Pool were, certainly, events of some importance. The school pony-cart, carrying ample provisions, took the Down road to the spot, but the girls, in twos and threes, or surrounding favourite mistresses, walked over the Downs as they listed, taking a longer and much more favourite way. An early start, before the greatest heat of the day, was arranged ; the return would be made after tea, when the glare had somewhat left the chalky ridges, and the sun was slowly setting, and the first owls were abroad. The hours between would be spent, according to individual choice, either in working magic at the Wishing Pool, collecting naturalist specimens, making rubbings from the old brasses in the little church which was one of the features of the district, taking snapshots, or amplifying Guide maps of the Downland round about. There was heaps to do, and the day would be all too short in the

opinion of every one of the girls, for all there
was to do. That the day might prove too long,
and too tiring also, for one individual among
them was the opinion, however, of Matron.

" But as for *you*, Josy, I hardly know what
to say. You'll never get there with that foot."

" Matron ! Oh, I *shall* ! Honest Injun, it
doesn't hurt a snap. I wouldn't *know* I had
an ankle. It's beautiful."

" By the time you've walked four miles, there
and back, you'll have it beautifully swollen
the size of two," Matron assured her. " It'll
be little under eight miles in all with the
running about you girls do between the walks.
Not that you're going to do it, as you'll find
out. You'll go down in the pony-cart if Miss
Heriot doesn't refuse. I'm just off to ask her.
Then you can use your ankle without trouble
when you get there."

" *Oh !* " Josy's face fell. On any other
occasion a drive with Miss Heriot would have
been an honour indeed. " And I was walking
with Sally ! "

It was to be their first walk since Josy's
return, and they were both looking forward to
it. The two weeks since half-term had been
too hot for rambles outside the school grounds.
Sally, therefore, had spent her rec.-times in
earnest tennis playing, and Josy had " practised

bowling," tennis being forbidden to her since her accident. Cricket was forbidden to her too, so far as making runs and fielding balls was concerned ; but with the firm intention of not wasting time in spite of that handicap, Josy had, on the advice of the cricket captain, decided to become a crack bowler if continual and careful practice could produce such a result. She and Hilary had spent almost every after-noon together, therefore, since the half-term, in a corner of the playing-field, working to that end.

" Well ? " Matron saw the dimple disappear from Josy's cheek and the disappointed colour mount instead. She deliberated as she went her way to Miss Heriot.

" Sally shall come too," decided the second mistress.

For Sally, in the opinion of every one on the staff, was no longer the rather unattractively bumptious specimen that she had seemed at first. " She's a different girl ; but, of course, what would you expect after nearly a term at Beech Trees ! " was the general opinion of the Mistresses' Room. Every one knew that there had been no trouble now with Sally for weeks, and that since Josy's return the pair had been much less together than they had been, rather anxiously, expected to be. That being the

case, and Sally seeming more taken up nowadays
with girls of her own age than with Josy, there
was no reason, in Miss Heriot's opinion, why
the pair should not spend part of the holiday
together.

Sally received the invitation with proper
expressions of appreciation. It was true that
she had been less with Josy lately, partly
because games and work kept them, perforce,
apart ; but partly, too, for another reason.
Sally was bothered still about the gipsies,
and, in spite of Sybil's announcement that she
herself could not possibly have been in any
way responsible for Perry's trouble, yet there
was a certain feeling of responsibility at the
back of her mind still. The gipsy man *had*
mentioned Perry. Suppose, then— But how !
Sally had worried and worried, and she was
still worrying in spite of all her efforts to con-
ceal the fact from Josy's keen eyes.

" I say, Sally, nothing up, is there ? "

" No," Sally forced herself to say. She
would have given loads to tell Josy her fears.
But she would have had to tell so much—about
the letter which Josy still thought to be safely
delivered on the day of her accident ; that it
was still in the gipsy folks' hands ; that the
Romany folk had haunted her again ; that they
had threatened ; and that the threat was **at**

the back of her mind always, because it had half seemed, even *then*, directed towards Perry, whereas *now*, when it was certain that he was in trouble from some unknown cause——

No, she would not tell Josy all this ; and yet she was sure that Josy, the keen, had begun to suspect that everything was not all right. So Sally had rather avoided solitary companionship with her small friend, just in case she should ask bang out some question which she herself might find mighty hard to answer. The invitation to drive down in the pony-cart was welcome, then, for with Miss Heriot as companion there would be no fear of Josy's possible questions on the way. Sally, looking rather relieved, took her seat in the pony-trap cheerily enough.

* * * * *

" But, old chap——"

" Here, stow it."

Perry was moodily gazing across the playing-field at Beeches. Pollitt was at his side.

" But it's such a regular ass's trick, yours, old chap ! What's the *matter* with just saying you don't know anything about those rotten notes and they can jolly well search for clues somewhere else ? What's the matter, I say ? " Pollitt's voice was urgent.

" Here, stow it."

" You jolly well needn't roar at a chap

anyway. After all, if any chap's got a right to ask you, *I* have. Didn't we go shares in those rotten pigeons, and a fine lot of bother they've made. And now, if you jolly well dry up whenever——"

" Here, stow it."

" It's not me that you need rave at ! I jolly well told the Head myself that you know nothing about 'em. And I truly believe, old chap, he's as pos. about it himself as I am. Only if you persist— Not gone off your nut, have you ? If you'd only say that you don't know anything about those rotten notes they found——"

" Here, stow it."

Perry continued to gaze moodily across the playing-field. Pollitt continued by his side.

CHAPTER XXIII

A PICNIC : A PATRIN : AND PERRY AGAIN

> " Oh, you'll tak' the low road,
>   And we'll tak' the high road,
>   But we'll reach the Wish Pool afore ye,"

chanted the laughing voices of the departing
girls up on the ridge, as they waved handker-
chiefs in farewell to Miss Heriot and her companions riding in state in the pony-trap below.

" Now we shan't see anything more of them,"
remarked the second mistress, endeavouring to
urge the pony to more vigorous steps with little
success. " Not for an hour or more. Dear
me, this pony's not called Dally for nothing.
Yes, it's a good five miles round to the Pool by
this road. They certainly will be there before
we arrive unless this chap mends his pace."

" Where does this road go to after the Pool,
Miss Heriot ? " asked Sally.

" On to Uckstead," the second mistress told
her. " And if to-day'd been last week we could
not have taken this road. It is always almost

impassable during that week of the year, for the Uckstead fair's quite an event. Round-abouts and merry-go-rounds ; side-shows galore too. In spite of the fact that it's supposed to be a horse fair there's always plenty of amusements going on, I believe. Fortunately, however, there's not a sign of any traffic now." Miss Heriot suddenly broke off and laughed. " I'm wrong in that statement, however," she went on. " See, girls ! If I hadn't inadvertently used the word ' sign,' perhaps I shouldn't have thought of it. But, look ! " She pointed with her whip.

At the side of the narrow roadway there lay, plain to see, nothing more important than a peeled branch of willow.

" It *mayn't* be ' sign,' but, again, it may be," said the second mistress, who acted also as captain of the Beech Trees Company of Guides. " And the reason I think it *may* be is this." She picked up a similar branch from the bottom of the trap. " I picked this up just outside the school gates," said Miss Heriot, " and thought some child had peeled it and thrown it down, But now, with that second one thrown over there, *and* with the knowledge that there's not any willow growing within a mile or so, so far as I can recall—and I know the district well—it seems to me, as a Guide—" Miss Heriot wrinkled up her brows and smiled. " We'll keep a look-out," suggested she, " for more And while you're looking out, think what you can make of it. Good practice, you know."

There was silence, save for the clip-clop of Dally's lazy hoofs, for a while. Then came a three-fold shout as they all, at one and the same instant, caught a glimpse of a third stripped branch of willow close to the ditch about a quarter-mile farther on.

" Fetch it, Sally, and we'll compare. See —yes, peeled just the same way, and stripped. No, go back again with it, and put it where you found it. If my wits had been a little quicker I should have left this first piece where it lay." Miss Heriot smiled. " It's ' sign,' certainly, I think. Some one has thrown down those branches on purpose. Gipsies, most likely, on their way to the fair."

" Oh, Miss Heriot," begged Josy, " is *that* a gipsy patrin ? "

" That's just what it is, Josy." Miss Heriot was looking as interested as the girls. " I've seen gipsies, as they worked at chair-making and baskets, throwing down handfuls of straw from their caravans. Evidently this willow has been left to show gipsy friends coming after them the way they have taken. Any number of gipsies meet at Uckstead horse fair

every year ; so many of them are horse-dealers,
you see. Not that those who left *this* ' sign '
are likely to have been, I rather think ; not
all of them, anyhow. They must have been
using willow for something or other——"

" Baskets ? " put in Sally promptly. " I
say, how awfully interesting. And one can
almost tell what part of the country they've
come from, can't one ? I mean, they're sure
to have travelled from somewhere where they
could get willow ? "

" That's perfectly right, Sally," said Miss
Heriot.

" Miss Heriot," Josy's voice broke in, " what
—I mean, what would the patrin be of gipsies
who made brooms for a living ? "

Josy wasn't looking at Sally, but her cheeks
were pink. She was thinking of the gipsy
woman on the Down. Sally knew that by the
sound of her voice. Miss Heriot, however,
evidently noticed nothing.

" Depends on what they were making their
brooms of, I should think. The Down gipsies
make them of heather, I believe. We have
some of them camping up here on the Down
every year. I haven't seen them this year."

Sally and Josy scanned the dusty road.

" Some people say that they camp in the
Hidden Ways," went on Miss Heriot ; " and

it seems quite a good idea. I suppose camps might easily be hidden there, and it would be much more sheltered. With an entrance of its own, too, perhaps." She urged on the reluctant Dally.

" Miss Heriot, where does the Hidden Ways lead to ? " inquired Sally, rather anxious to change the topic.

It was supposed, Miss Heriot told them— at least so the guide-books said—to lead right across the Down from the sea a few miles on. The smugglers had used it long ago.

" It opens out, I believe, in several places— quite easy to find if one had time to search," said the second mistress ; " but probably there is a main exit somewhere, and there are generally rules about the ways and byways of these places. Reasons, too—" Miss Heriot laughed. " I dare say there are some smugglers' secrets about the Hidden Ways which no one knows or will know," she said. " Look ! I see the ' Cosy ' is still shut up," she went on, pointing with her whip.

There stood the little house, looking to Josy's sympathetic eyes dreadfully unhappy and lonely in the middle of its flowery garden. Mary's clothes-line was still up between two apple-trees as though waiting for garments which were to have been washed on the day that the bad news came. But there was no smoke from the chimney, and the windows were shuttered. Mary had gone home for a while to her mother until Joe's innocence should be proved.

" I expect the little house has had other queer experiences," said Miss Heriot. " It is supposed to have been the home of that old smuggler who lies in the so-called Haunted Tomb in our churchyard. Sally, you will have heard all our eerie stories by now ? "

" Yes, Miss Heriot ; in the dorm." Sally woke from a reverie. She had been thinking of their gipsies again. Naturally enough, of course, since it had happened that the very subject which was never far from her thoughts had been so curiously brought up again by Miss Heriot herself. Sally knew, too, that Josy must have been thinking of their gipsies too, because of the question she had asked about a broom-making gipsy's " patrin." But one of Miss Heriot's remarks had remained in Sally's memory, and had caused her a sudden pang of apprehension. The second mistress had said, quite casually, that most gipsies went to the horse fair, and that some of them were horse-dealers. It was from the fair, Sally suddenly remembered, that Mary said Joe had brought back his notes. Had he got them from the gipsies ? Oh, but if so—well, then, how could Perry come in to the trouble ? The half-idea seemed worse than no clue. Sally abandoned it with a sigh just as Miss Heriot pulled in the pony with a jerk.

" Here, you two," said the second mistress, " I really think we'll pamper Dally for this half-mile uphill ; he seems to imagine himself a regular martyr, and certainly the weight of the lunch must be considerable. The slope's gradual, Josy, and it won't hurt your leg."

" Sally," began Josy, as soon as they were alone, " Sally—I say, *Sally !* I do jolly well wish you'd tell me—*is* anything up ? "

" ' *Up* ' ? " repeated Sally.

" Yes—rows, I mean, or anything ? Anything I don't know. Sally, it's absolutely rotten if you don't tell me." Josy gave a little gasp. " I'm sure there is, and I jolly well wish you'd tell me. I'm not so bad at helping, you know," continued Josy. " You *did* say I was of some use ! "

" Rows—no," began Sally.

" And even if I did get a ' throw ' it was just at the end," pursued Josy eagerly. " And you know I did think out some good plans, didn't I ? Not that I haven't wished and wished that I'd never been such a juggins as to send that pigeon-post letter. That started everything. But—well, it did *end* all right, you know, and we *have* kept rules all right ever since; and, Sally, I say you might tell me—only you needn't, really, because I know there is ! *Is* anything up ? "

" Well," remarked Sally, alarmed by an ominous note in Josy's generally cheery tone, " look here— I say," she went on, " it's—er —nothing much—at least, probably it's nothing at all. It's that I've been thinking, and— Josy, be a sport, and don't ask again."

" Only one thing," urged Josy, going straight to the bull's-eye, " then I won't, honest Injun. *Is* it about the letter, Sally, eh ? "

Sally couldn't help the tell-tale colour in her cheeks.

" It is. *Oh !* " Josy gave a little run forward. " And—I've promised not to ask anything more ! Sally, you'd tell *me* first, wouldn't you, if there was anything that I could do to help ? "

" Rather, kid." Sally gave her paw a friendly grip. She would have liked nothing better than at that moment to make Josy her confidante again. But she wasn't going to. Josy was, somehow, more now to Sally than just a safety-valve. Sally had made up her mind to worry through this particular bother by herself. She quickened her steps, and with

Josy's hand still in hers they hurried together after the pony-trap, which was waiting for them at the top of the hill.

* * * * *

" Then, Perry, you have nothing further to tell me about the notes ? "

" No, sir."

" Pollitt, who owned the pigeons with you, declares that you can know nothing about them." The Head's voice was level. " But you own that the pigeons did carry the notes found in your desk ? "

" Yes, sir."

" And Hinnigan ? "

" Sir, I'm as positive as I can be that *he's* innocent."

" But it was he who managed your pigeon-post. Have you any idea, Perry—I ask you to think before you reply to me—*how* those notes came to you ? "

" Yes, sir ; but that's all I can say."

" You realize that by those words you might yourself come under suspicion of knowing more than you should ? "

" Yes, sir ; but that's all I can say."

CHAPTER XXIV

JOSY AND THE WISHING POOL

" HULLO!" remarked Hilary. She hastened forward with a grin of greeting, as though she and Josy had been separated for years. She had been standing with a crowd of others, all girls older than herself and most of them members of Miss Heriot's own form, who had volunteered for the honour of helping to unburden their class-mistress's load upon her arrival with the lunch on board. As Dally toiled up the grassy path, trying to give the impression by his feeble bearing that, if any one was in need of nourishment it was he himself, the wagonette and its occupants were surrounded by the troop.

" Josy, hop out. Sally, you may as well wait and help with the harness "—Miss Heriot was giving directions—" while we unpack."

" You're *my* partner now, Josy," remarked Hilary with unction. " Come on, too. There's lots of things to do. To begin with, Daphne

wants to snap our form. They're waiting till
you come, and it's the last film on her roll.
And then—" They raced off, Josy casting
one backward glance in the direction of Sally's
stooping figure.

" What about the Wishing Pool ? " she inquired as they ran.

For she had made up her mind as to one
thing during the latter part of the drive. Sally
had owned to being worried in some way connected—though how *could* it be ? Josy wondered
—with the gipsy letter. Well, there was one
thing, so Josy told herself, that she could do
to help—there was the Wishing Pool. She
remembered that Mary had once won that
competition prize on the very evening after
they had returned from the grotto. Some one
else, too, had declared, Josy recalled eagerly,
that, although an aunt had certainly paid for
her last bicycle, yet, in the opinion of its for-
tunate recipient, it was just as much the gift
of the magic pool ! Josy herself had, until an
hour go, fully intended to wish a certain wish
connected with cricket—that she should get
into the Second Eleven next year in spite of
this year's ankle handicap. She and Hilary,
co-conspirators in the matter, had decided
that morning, just as soon as the picnic-place
of the day had been announced, that their

wishes should be identical and the same. But now——

" We've all wished," Hilary was telling her excitedly. " We wished straight off. We all went in together. It was tremendous fun. It was so hot when we got here that one of the mistresses said it would be the coolest thing to do : because it's always cool in the grotto, and out of the sun. I wished my wish ; but I'll come with you for yours, Josy, of course."

Josy hesitated. It had certainly been arranged between the pair of them that they should brave the magic together. Both of them, though they would have scorned to own the fact to each other, were rather in awe of the grotto with its silences and tree-sighings. It was entered by a tiny parting in the bushes, and seemed almost roofed in with the thick boughs of trees which met overhead, and which seemed to have something sinister about them, somehow, Josy always felt. To-day, however— well, Josy had changed her mind about her dearest wish of all, and she hoped it would not be difficult to make Hilary understand.

" I say, Hil, if you don't mind—" she began.

Hilary didn't mind at all, she said, when Josy had explained that, for reasons which truly she couldn't possibly divulge even to Hilary, her wish was changed.

" I'll have to simply slog and stodge at cricket," said Josy, " instead of wishing. Perhaps it will do instead. But anyhow, whether it does or doesn't, I've got another wish now —a tremendously private one too, I'm afraid. I'll be absolutely bound—honest Injun, I will —to go in alone."

" Right," agreed Hilary, trying not to be as curious as she was beginning to fear she might become in the matter. " We'll go this instant and get it over, and I'll wait just beyond the bushes with my ears simply bunged up tight so that I couldn't possibly hear, but not at all far away, though, you know."

Josy squeezed her hand gratefully—for the grotto *was* eerie. One had to wish one's wish aloud, too, so it was necessary, if it was a secret one, to go there unaccompanied. " Let's go and get it over," suggested she.

Easier said than done. As they crossed the ridge a perfect bevy of juniors burst upon them, headed by the redoubtable Daphne of the camera.

" Josy ! Josy ! Josy ! If you knew the ages we've waited to get our form together. I want this snap particularly for a birthday present for Miss Grant, and it's my last film."

Josy and Hilary, perforce, therefore fell into

line amiably enough, and spent the next half-
hour in waiting for the sun to come out and
in arranging their faces to suit the autocrat of
the camera.

" *There !* " Daphne decided with a sigh,
just as a hurrying prefect burst upon them all.

" Here, all of you, fetch some more wood
for the fire, please. We haven't half enough,
and we shan't have enough unless every one
of you juniors help. Leave what you're
doing till after lunch ! " Josy and Hilary found
themselves flying in every direction, searching
for sticks and breathlessly carrying them fire-
wards. The Wishing Pool was certainly not
to be visited until later on.

" Never mind," whispered Hilary, " we'll
get there. It will be utterly private, too.
We'll go as soon as lunch is over."

Something else came in the way then—a
suddenly suggested ramble to the wild strawberry patch on the other side of the Down.

" A good thing that you drove down, Josy,"
smiled Miss Shirley, who had suggested the
idea, " for you couldn't have managed the
walk otherwise. However, we'll start after
lunch, and be back in plenty of time for tea."

Very jolly, of course. Josy wanted to go
as much as any other of the juniors. Only
Hilary understood the look on her face.

" I say, Josy, we'll wangle it after tea. Honest
Injun, we will."

They did too. When the afternoon ramble
was over, and when the picnic tea was finished,
while the older girls were washing up the tea-
things and arranging them in the baskets, there
came a possible time. Hilary and Josy looked
at each other and started off.

"Hil-ary!"—it was Miss Heriot's voice calling—"one minute. Come here from wherever
you're going. I want to speak to you."

"I *must* go. But I'll come after you. Don't
wait, or they'll be telling us to start. You
don't—" "Funk" Hilary had almost said,
though not quite. But Josy had understood.
The almost-said word shamed her, and she
pulled herself together.

Funk! As if she'd let herself. She hurried on alone. She *must* wish that wish for
Sally!

Tea had lasted long, and the shadows,
lengthy and dim, were beginning to creep over
the Downs as she crossed the ridge. Almost
like the shadows of ghostly smugglers of long
ago they seemed. It would be more spooky-
feeling still in the grotto, Josy knew, as she
set her teeth ; for even in daytime it was
quietly dim there, and the overhead trees, even
at noonday, sighed in a magicky kind of way,

as though deciding, so Josy always thought, whether or not they would grant each wish.

But this particular wish should not be lost for any cowardice of her own, Josy declared, setting her straight little back still straighter. She made her way over the quiet turf, and reached the bushes. It was as she passed through, leaving the light of the summer evening behind her, leaving the sound of the girls' voices too, and entering a gloom which made her shiver a little in spite of herself as she went, that suddenly her ears caught a sound. Was it the soughing of the strange trees overhead? No. It was more than that. Some one was there in the dim grotto besides herself.

Josy's first idea was that it must be one of the girls, here on the same kind of errand as she was herself—to voice, perhaps, some wish which she had not wanted to utter in the general chorus. She was turning to go back and leave the first-comer in possession, when suddenly her mind changed, and she forgot everything as the sound of sobs caught her ear.

Bitter sobs, loud and uncontrolled. And words with them—words which, strangely enough, Josy could not understand. Some other language than her own. Was this some dreadful kind of magic? She would have turned to go back if it had not been that evidently, quite evidently, some one was unhappy. Therefore, frightened or not frightened, Josy knew that she must stay.

" I say," she began in a gaspy chirp, " *I'm* here, you know, whoever you are ! "

If she had been surprised before, she was rendered almost dizzy with fear for one instant after she had uttered those words. There came a sudden swirl of garments through the gloom, and a figure threw itself at her feet. But at the sound of the next words Josy began to understand.

" *Oh ! oh !* Sure, it's the little gentle rawnee. The little lucky rawnee ! And me just wishing for her ! "

The gipsy woman ! It could be nobody else. Josy gave a little gasp, partly with surprise at seeing her again, partly with relief, and partly with wonder at her words.

" *Me !* But you couldn't have been wanting to see me, you know," said Josy. " And why are you crying ? Oh, I do hope your darling baby isn't ill ? "

But at the mention of the baby's name the gipsy woman's sobs became once more uncontrolled. The little thing *was* ill—very ill. There was no luck for the poor baby, so she sobbed, none at all. That was why she was

there ; she had come to wish for it to get well.
She had seen all the gay young rawnees with
the light hearts wishing—yes, from among the
bushes she had watched them. But her own
gentle little rawnee who had kissed the baby
and brought it luck, her own gentle rawnee,
hadn't come ! And so the sobs went on.

" I was driving," Josy told her gently.
" But I've come now. I've come here on purpose to wish."

" Little rawnee, then "—the gipsy woman
was on her knees before her—" will ye wish
health, rawnee, for the baby ? 'Twill sure
bring her luck, rawnee, if yer do. Sure, black
luck, rawnee dear, black luck has followed
the poor Romany folk up at the camp in the
Hidden Ways where ye came." The gipsy
woman crouched down in the grotto at Josy's
feet, rocking herself to and fro.

CHAPTER XXV

JOSY CHANGES HER WISH

"BUT, you see, I don't quite think I *can*—" began Josy.

The grotto was dim about her, but she had no thought at all now of the eeriness of the place. She had forgotten everything in the trouble of the gipsy woman at her side—everything except that Sally was in trouble too.

"I've promised—at least, I've promised inside me, you know," said Josy, "and that's exactly the same thing, really. I've a friend who's in trouble too. Why, you know her, of course." Josy suddenly stopped short and gasped. For the gipsy woman would understand: it was to her own camp in the Hidden Ways that she and Sally had ridden to buy back that letter about which Sally seemed still in some strange mysterious trouble. "I almost think I could explain to you," went on Josy. "You see, you know about it. I'm dreadfully sorry about your baby, and I'd love to wish for it to get better. I'm sure, too, that Sally would tell me to, if she were here. But—" She was beginning to decide that, perhaps, if she could only go and bring Sally, they might both wish together, when suddenly the Romany woman clutched her by her arm.

" ' Sal-lee,' you say ? The rawnee with the proud heart and the cold eye? Sure, the Romanies keep far from her, though they would always be kind to *you*, little rawnee. You mean ' Sara Heath'?" Her voice was almost frightened.

"Yes. But how did you know? Why— But, of course, her name was on that letter. It's about the letter that she's so worried, and I'd meant to wish—" Josy was going on, but the gipsy burst suddenly into a breathless torrent of words.

" Oh, oh ! It was that, sure, which has brought the luck—the bad, black luck—on my baby, yes. 'Twas to himself that I said it. ' Give the rawnee back her letter, Manfrey,' I said, ' or black luck will fall on us. Sure, there's no harm nor hurt in drookering of them for a silver bit; but this is different, in course it is. Only georgeos or mumpers would serve the rawnees so, Manfrey.' Sure, I ses it; and we's Romanies of true blood."

" But I don't think I understand what you

mean," interrupted Josy, staring. " The letter, I thought——"

" But so set he was," the woman's voice flowed on, " and now to goodness, rawnee, I don't know, sure, what he done with it. He've got it, plain he have. Same as he'd got it, Manfrey had, the day we come up to the proud rawnee by the fence. Held her head high, she did, and said we'd cheated of her. Sure, that wasn't what Manfrey'd meant not to do at all, no. But another few shilluns was all what he arsted for. And when she names him names, him being a Romany of true blood, why, he called down ill-luck on her. ' Give her back her letter, Manfrey,' I begs and prays, ' or the black luck 'twill be on us ourselves, sure.' But not a word would Manfrey say 'cept that he do better wi' the letter, rawnee, than that. As close shut as a beech-mast my man can be, rawnee ; but, sure, for the baby's sake, he'll tell me now. I'll arst him to-night, rawnee, and get the letter back for ye. Sure, I will."

Josy was listening, wide-eyed in the gloom. It was no good asking the gipsy woman questions, she was too unhappy to listen ; the flow of talk was easing her troubled heart. And, besides, Josy was beginning to understand quite well how matters lay. The gipsies had evidently never given back the letter. That was the reason why Sally was looking so bothered. The gipsies had kept the letter, and it had brought them ill-luck, as the gipsy woman said. Josy didn't wonder. " But it isn't fair for the *baby* to have the bad luck," she said, thinking her thoughts aloud.

For answer the woman began to sob in earnest. " No, no, little dear rawnee. No. Oh, little rawnee, sure you's the little lucky lovely lady wot speaks truth like the birds. An' ef ye'll wish fer health fer him, here at the Wishing Pool, rawnee, w'y, then, the luck will turn, sure. Listen here, rawnee, too : 'twill change the luck fer yer high rawnee friend too, sure, an' so it will. For ef ye'll come around to the camp, rawnee, where ye comed afore, I'll have the letter ready and waitin' for ye to-night. Himself won't refuse it after what ye've done for the baby, Manfrey won't."

Josy stood perfectly still. She had made up her mind already to change her wish again. For she was quite certain that Sally would want her to. Babies were so small, Josy remembered, and the gipsy baby had been so very small and sweet, with such big black laughing eyes, that Josy couldn't bear to think of its being ill and unhappy. " No, it wasn't fair for the baby to have the bad luck. And besides "—Josy gave a little gasp as she remem-

bered. " Truly, it's all been my fault," she
thought. " Even the baby's being ill too ;
for it's all wound up together. It was all
because of me that the letter ever got sent by
that pigeon from Mary's. Sally said so outside the church, and though she was too kind
to mean it really, yet it's true. That's why I
thought out the runaway canter ; I thought
that would set everything right. But it hasn't ;
and so it's because of me, still, that the baby's
ill and that Sally's unhappy too. Oh, what
shall I do ? "

As though in answer came the gipsy's voice.
" Little gracious rawnee, sure, don't be sorrow-
ful," she said gently. " Give a wish for the
baby, and, sure, your own troubles shall blow,
too, like the mists at mornin'. Ef ye'll just step
up to the camp to-night, why, sure, there shall
be no mistakenness, rawnee darling, for my man
will listen to me now, and give me the letter,
and willing, when I tells him that you wished
here for the baby's sake."

" I'll do that. Of course, I'd meant to.
Wish for the baby, I mean," said Josy with a
little gulp. " Sally would tell me to. She's
not proud, like you say. I know she would."
But her voice sounded very grave as she bent
over the pool where so many voices had chanted
their wishes laughingly that afternoon. " I

wish," said Josy, " that the darling gipsy baby may get well, and that the bad luck may go."

She felt herself clasped close in warm gipsy arms and kissed with full red gipsy lips as she uttered the last words, while gipsy tears fell on her own pink cheeks.

" Oh, 'tis you yourself, rawnee darling, that shall have love, and luck, and favour. Oh, 'tis you——"

" But "—Josy's voice sounded as desolate as she felt—" it's Sally that I'm thinking about. She's so unhappy, and you see I haven't done anything at all to help *her*."

"Sure, then, little rawnee dear "—the gipsy woman's voice was kind—" come ye to the camp to-night, like I ses to ye. Himself's away till evenin' with the gryengros, but he'll be back 'fore night. And then I'll say, ' Manfrey, the little gentle rawnee wot brought the luck back and wished for the baby at the Pool, she's a-comin' to-night to the camp, Manfrey. Not the haughty rawnee wot upbraided of you, Manfrey,' I'll say, ' but the little gentle rawnee wot come with her and kissed luck to the baby. And for the baby's sake, then, and for the sake of the little gentle rawnee-with-the-singing-bird-of-love-at-her-heart, Manfrey,' I'll say, ' you'll give me the letter now, eh ? you being a Romany chel of true blood !

And, sure, he'll do that same. I knows the ways of 'im, rawnee, and I knows the love in his heart, rawnee, for the baby. And you'll be going back, a-stepping over the Down with light heart, an' with the letter in your hand, rawnee, for your high friend," continued the gipsy woman garrulously, " and the luck will be brought again for the high rawnee, and the luck will turn for us Romanies too, when the letter gets to its rightful owner. Sure, 'tis the letter brought the black luck to us all, rawnee dear."

" I truly believe it did," Josy was beginning, " but—" She deliberated rather anxiously, for another visit to the camp would mean another breach of rules. And the result of the last visit had been dreadful enough. Josy had found the pain easy to bear because of the certainty she had felt all the while that now everything was quite all right again : that Sally had the letter, and that rules might be kept now comfortably at Beech Trees " for ever and ever."

But matters had gone dreadfully and miserably wrong after all. Sally was still unhappy ; the letter was still with the gipsies : if it were to be got back again rules must be broken yet again.

" But—" began Josy again, just as an urgent call came suddenly from outside the grotto.

" Jo-seee ! Jo-*seee !* " It was Hilary's loud
voice. " Aren't you finished yet ? You *are*
there still, aren't you ? Inside the grotto, I
mean. May I come in ? "

" I'll be waitin' for ye, rawnee dear, with
the letter, sure, to-night, when the sun's
down. I'm away back there now." The
woman glided into the shadows just as Hilary
burst through the opening.

" O-oh ! it *is* dark in here, isn't it ? Oh,
Josy, I was afraid something had happened,"
she began in a breathless whisper. " Oh,
come out. Your wish *must* have been a jolly
long one." They were through the entrance
now. " Miss Heriot called me back to say
that *I'm* to drive back with you and her in the
trap to-night. Isn't it scrum ? Sally's walking
back with Sheila. And then Miss Heriot said
would I help catch Dally ? And he simply
wouldn't be caught. Then she said to fetch
you, and—why, Josy, whatever's up ? "

" Nothing—or, at least, I'd rather not say,
I think," said Josy in as offhand a tone as she
could muster.

" You didn't see anything magicky, or anything like that, did you ? " inquired Hilary in
a half - whisper, looking over her shoulder
grotto - wards in an apprehensive manner.
" *Oh !* "

"What is it?" inquired Josy, refraining from turning too.

"It's—oh, nothing magical, of course; but there's one of those gipsies—the broom-selling ones. She's been about all day, staring from the heather, the girls say, and looking at them each in turns. And Miss Heriot said that perhaps she's lost her camp and is looking for another. Miss Heriot said that they're quite nice gipsies, but that the police are moving them all on, because of the counterfeit notes, or something. So they're not to stay on the Down, and they're all going away. I've a good mind to tell Miss Heriot on the way home that this woman——"

"I say!" Josy suddenly clutched Hilary's arm. "Listen. She a perfectly nice gipsy, absolutely. And you're not to say anything to Miss Heriot about her, because——" Josy stopped.

Hilary, as was natural, waited with eagerness for the completion of the sentence.

"Because she's a sort of a friend of mine, I suppose," finished up Josy lamely; "and it might make things horribly and absolutely all wrong if you do."

CHAPTER XXVI

JOSY MAKES UP HER MIND

JOSY made up her mind on the way home that she *would* go to the camp. It suddenly occurred to her, while seated in the trap, half-listening to the voluble chatter which Hilary was addressing to the second mistress, and half-watching the rise and fall of Dally's lazy hoofs in the dust of the road, that there was another aspect of the case hitherto unrealized.

Hilary had said that the gipsies were being moved on from their camps. Well, any day the gipsies camping in the Hidden Ways might have to go—at any hour, the gipsy man, and the baby, and the gipsy woman too. And then? Well, after *that*, of course, it would be impossible to get the letter back, and Sally would continue to look unhappy and to hold herself aloof. Oh yes, in spite of rules, in spite of her own feelings, in spite of everything, Josy must go to the camp for the letter to-night.

" It's absolutely my own fault that it's there, really," she reminded herself; "and this time Sally shan't break rules too. I wouldn't break them if I possibly could help it, but——"

It was queer that at that moment Hilary's loud tones broke most opportunely into her thoughts.

" Miss Heriot, we'll be allowed to talk in dorms. to-night, won't we ?—it being a holiday, you know."

" Oh yes, Hilary. No rules till to-morrow."

"No rules till to-morrow !" Suddenly Josy's heart felt lighter again. Perhaps it wouldn't be so dreadfully un-Beech Treesy if she went, so long as to-night was chosen for the expedition. No rules would be broken, and that would make every difference. She wouldn't mind—for she wouldn't *let* herself mind—the lonely journey to the Hidden Ways after dusk. She wouldn't dread—for she wouldn't *let* herself dread—the secret visit to the camp : it would put everything right again for Sally.

For Josy had quite realized that the woman meant to keep her word this time. She had been genuinely grateful and thankful, and her kiss had been a loving one. " She'll have it ready for me herself, and I dare say I shan't see that man with the shifty eyes. And she'll let me go back quick, I shouldn't wonder, 'cos

I'll ask her. If the baby's better she might even walk a little way with me," thought Josy eagerly ; " and I dare say I'll get back before the owls and the bats and those beetles-with-wings are too much about."

But, for all her heartening-up thoughts, her face was a very white and tired one as she sat there thinking gravely in the trap.

" Very tired, Josy ? " inquired Miss Heriot. " Is your ankle troubling you ? "

" Not a single scrap, thank you, Miss Heriot," Josy assured her eagerly. " And I'm not one bit tired either."

But, all the same, on arrival at school Matron appeared to have her own ideas on the subject of Josy, the late invalid. " Josy, you're to go straight to bed now ; yes, I agree with Miss Heriot, you *have* overtired yourself. And you might as well have your own bed in the San. for to-night, then you can sleep straight through without the other girls wakening you with all their noise coming up. *I* know what holidays are ! " Josy found herself following Matron upstairs, feeling terribly perturbed and anxious. She had meant to slip out of the cloakroom while the others were dancing. She could not do that now.

" Matron, please. Truly ! "

" Into bed you get, Josy ; and here's your

supper-tray. It's trifle and chicken, same as
the rest are getting, and eat it up. You'll be
asleep in half an hour, which would not be the
case in your own dorm. to-night, what with no
rules and all that gibberish." Matron was
gone. She returned when, the supper eaten,
Josy, in her professional opinion, was ready
to be tucked up and left. " Now you couldn't
be dancing, you know," she told her admon-
ishingly, " so why lie there and worry ? "

But it was not thoughts of the dancing,
even now in progress of being carried out in
the hall below, that had brought the crinkles
to Josy's forehead. Everybody was down
there, of course—even Miss Dean honoured
holiday dances with her presence for the opening waltz, and sailed off on the arm of a stiff
and gallant Sixth Form girl. All the mistresses would be there, of course, as Josy knew,
and the girls to a maiden. Probably half the
kitchen staff would be watching, too, from the
gallery. Holiday dances were always a feature
of great days at Beech Trees, and however
many miles the girls and mistresses might
have tramped or cycled, it never appeared
to make the least difference to their dancing
powers at night. On any other holiday, certainly, Josy might have lain feeling terribly
rebellious at being shut out of Paradise, but

to-night other things crowded even holiday matters from her mind.

The camp! She'd got to get there. The gipsies might be moved on to-morrow. Why, the gipsy woman herself had specially told her to come to-night. " Perhaps she knew," thought Josy, " that they were off. Oh, how can I manage it ? "

It was while she lay wondering, with the strains of the " Coal Black Mammy " floating up from the hall, played with all the verve and fury that Dulcie could put into it, that Josy suddenly had an idea.

Why, being sent to bed like this need not make things more difficult! It might make things easier—much. Josy tiptoed across the bare floor and peeped through the window. She could get out by the San. balcony and down the stone steps to the garden as easy as anything! She would, too. She would, because she really *must*. Why, she could slip on her things and be off now, and in less than two hours' time, before the school was asleep, she'd be back again. Of course she would— with Sally's letter. The gipsy woman had said " after sundown." She had said that the man was away until then. Josy's decision was made.

Below, in the hall, the strains of the " Fox-

trot Ball " were being gaily hammered out by
Miss Shirley as Josy tiptoed off. She hated
tiptoeing ; she hated with every bit of her
having to go without asking leave ; she hated
to know that there still were secrets and mysteries and rule-breakings. It was all so un-
Beech Treesy, and she had thought all that
part of things was over on the day when Sally
and she had ridden to the camp. However,
she owed it to Sally to get the letter ; it was
through her, Josy, that all this trouble had
been caused, she told herself. Just as soon as
Sally got it back again there would be no more
clouds on Sally's brow ; no secrets that she
might not share.

" She hasn't told me because she's a
brick ; but oh, I'm so glad that I found out
everything after all," thought Josy as she
started off.

It wasn't until she had left the garden—
until the last strains of the piano had died
away—that suddenly the evening seemed to
close round her. It hadn't seemed evening,
not even up in the San., in bed. Josy had
felt like the little boy in her *Child's Garden of
Verses* who " had to go to bed by day," lying
there with the sound of the girls' merry-
making below. It had seemed daytime still
in the garden. It was only as she crossed the

grassy roadway and reached the Down that she felt the difference.

Gone was the glare of the sun. The Downs seemed shadowy ; the green of the turf was deeper ; the far-away blue of the sea was deeper ; the blue of the sky above was the deep, deep blue of a summer night. There were the bedtime cries of birds sounding now and then ; timid, anxious notes they seemed. Rustles in the bushes meant birds, of course ; but they made Josy hurry very fast. Rabbits were abroad, too ; and the call of the sheep over the Downs sounded faint and far away and sadly mysterious somehow. Josy quickened her steps. It really wasn't very far, she told herself.

She felt tired, though, after the efforts of the day, and that made the way seem longer than she had expected. The holiday had been the longest outing since the accident. She hadn't realized, until now, how tired she really was. Well, it wouldn't take long now, she told herself, after half-an-hour's run. The camp was not far—just over the ridge where the clumps of bushes stood which hid the Hidden Ways. It was just close to some gorse bushes, which weren't showing their gold at all in this dim light. " Perhaps the darkness hides it for them," thought Josy, " for fear the Down gnomes steal it. I suppose that at night they'd

be all about." She tried to hearten herself
up by singing as she went,—

> " Bathing in a dew-pond
> Is the greatest fun.
> But wait till the chill is off
> The dew, or you're sure to cough."

And——

She broke off. " Oh, *there's* the right patch,
and I'm really and truly here ! "

She certainly had reached the spot, but there
was no sign of the gipsy woman waiting for her.

" I hope the baby's not worse," thought Josy
anxiously. " Well, any way, I know them
well enough now to go straight in, I think."
She made a little dive through the bushes and
crept in. It was then, as she crept through
the place where the gipsy woman's face had
peeped up at them that first time, that Josy
suddenly gasped. What was wrong ? For
there was no smoke coming up from the bushes
as had always been the case before ; there
were no sounds of voices, no noise of barking
dogs, no baby cries to meet her ears as formerly.
The entrance to the Hidden Ways was as quiet
as the Down itself over which she had hurried.
Quieter, perhaps—or it seemed so—with the
memory of the noisy clatter which Josy had
expected to hear again still in her mind.

The camp had been moved on !

Until that moment Josy didn't realize how much she had depended on the gipsies at the camp for keeping the solitude of the Downs at bay. Now it seemed to close round her, as before her yawned the empty space, with its odds and ends strewed around as though there had been a hurried departure. Fear, which she couldn't easily throw off, clutched Josy's heart.

They were gone ; she was all alone, out on the Down ! And Sally's letter ! Was that gone too ? Had they cheated her again ? " I will not be an idjut and think of spooky things," thought Josy with chattering teeth. " I don't believe the woman cheated me. Her eyes were true as true. Could she have left it for me ? Oh, if so——"

It was as she bent down among the litter of camp remains that her quick eyes caught sight, in the gloaming, of something on the ground at her feet.

CHAPTER XXVII

WHERE IS JOSY ?

ROLL, at Beech Trees, was called at eight o'clock on ordinary nights ; on holidays an extra hour was always granted to the school. Supper had been taken at seven o'clock on the evening of the long-remembered Oxford-Results-Whole ; dancing had followed on in the big hall. For an hour and a half mistresses had succeeded mistresses, girls had succeeded girls in cheerful alacrity on the piano stool. Tunes as archaic as the " Valse Bleu " and the " Tin Gee-gee Polka " had been as gaily greeted as the more modern products of " Swanee " and " Hesitation." The girls were not particular—anything was worth dancing that took them on to the well-polished floor with a partner. There were no such things as wall-flowers on these occasions, for mistresses, however weary and footsore they might be, always gallantly rose from their seats to take pity upon small partnerless ones, and pre-

tended not to mind when their evening slippers
were tramped upon by earnest and energetic
feet. It was not until the ten-minutes' bell
had sounded to warn every one that roll-time
was close at hand that the dancers showed any
signs of fatigue.

There would be just time for " Sir Roger "
now. Partners for this particular dance, which
was always the grand final of a holiday, had
been decided long ago. Every mistress had
been approached by the head of her respective
form, and Miss Dean, who had opened the
proceedings by waltzing with the head girl,
always closed them by dancing " Sir Roger "
with the youngest girl in the school. It was
just as the company had arranged their lines
—just as Sybil, at the piano, had sounded the
loud and crashing chord which was intended
to announce to all and sundry that the last
dance of the evening was ready to begin, that
the unexpected happened.

Nothing more nor less than the dramatically
startling appearance upon the scene of Matron !
Bearing a sick-room tray, which added to the
incongruous effect of her appearance, she
advanced with a mien that suggested, almost,
that of Lady Macbeth in the sleep-walking
scene. She had entered suddenly by the small
door at the platform entrance of the hall, and,

without a look or word, swept swiftly through the lines of waiting dancers. Sybil, at the piano, sat and stared at the apparition, and played no further note. Girls and mistresses gave way to allow Matron to pass on, as though she had been Cæsar himself, unchecked to where the headmistress stood.

Then came an instant in which the whole school stood amazed—something was evidently up, but what was it?—while Matron spoke in a sepulchral whisper in Miss Dean's ear.

That instant was followed by another, during which the Head, with a courteous but abstracted bow of apology to her small partner, turned to accompany the unexpected arrival from the hall.

And then, " Sybil, please "—Miss Heriot stepped in without an instant's hesitation— " we are waiting for ' Sir Roger.' "

Crash ! came the first loud chord.

The dance began, but everybody danced that dance vaguely, and in the brief instants during which partners met partners the same question hovered on everybody's lips,—

" Whatever is it ? "

Even the announcement at the end of the dance that a special concession had been allowed of an extra half-hour in hall, and that Miss Dean would take prayers at half-past nine instead of at the hour, though met with a show of acclamation, was just as certainly understood to imply still more plainly that "something" was up !

"It's not a fire, is it ? " shivered a junior to her companion during the interval.

"Or could it be anything to do with Mary and the notes ? "

It occurred to nobody—not even to Sally— that the dramatic entry of Matron might be connected in any way with Josy upstairs.

For Sally had hardly seen Josy all day, not since the drive of the morning. Circumstances had kept them apart. On arrival at the picnicking place Sally herself had been haled, even while unharnessing Dally, to join a contingent composed of members of her own form who were off to see the tiny Down church a mile away and take rubbings of the brasses there. After lunch she had found herself pressed to join another expedition who were keen to explore elsewhere. All her companions had already "wished" at the Pool before her late arrival, and since that was the case Sally was too matter-of-fact to think it necessary to go there. She had tramped back over the Down in the evening with Hesther and Dorothy after one of the jolliest days she remembered since she had come.

It would have been utterly jolly, she reflected, but for the fact that there'd been, all
the time, that gloom of uncertainty and bother-
ment at the back of things ; just as there
always was. Still, Josy's questions had been
carefully staved off. Sally didn't think the
kid suspected anything, really.

" And I'll take jolly good care she doesn't,"
she thought, gritting her teeth as she danced.
" But, after all, I dare say I'm getting fussy.
Sybil thought so anyway.   I expect the
gipsies tore up the letter ; and whether they
did or didn't, it couldn't possibly bring Perry
into a row so far as I can see. Sybil as
much as said so anyway.   How could his
bothers be anything to do with me ?   But I
wish——"

It was at that instant that Matron had entered unawares.   It was not until half an hour
later that the bombshell fell—on the girls,
at least.

" I wish to speak to all of you."   They were
in their lines now, arranged for prayers and
roll, and the Head had entered in her usual
quiet way.   Her voice was as level as ever, too,
but her eyes looked anxious and worried.   " I
wish to know if any one of you can help us.
Josy, who went straight to bed on her return
from the picnic, is not in the Sanatorium now.

She has evidently dressed and left the building,
for, after half-an-hour's search, we can find
no trace of her here. Before taking further
steps, then, I wish to ask you all : Can any
of you throw any light on the reason of her
disappearance ? "

There was a pause. Every eye looked
straight at the headmistress.

Sally felt her heart give a huge leap. " *Josy !* "
Oh, whatever could this mean ?

" None of you know anything ? " The
Head's voice was very anxious. " It is most
unlike Josy to break rules in any way ; but
she has lately been ill. To-day she was very
quiet and unlike herself, I hear, during the
drive home. So if any of you have a suggestion
to make——"

No one spoke.

" Who was with her during the day ? You,
Sara Heath, I believe ? "

" I drove down with her in the trap. I
don't think——" Sally hardly recognized her
voice. She was cudgelling her brains. *Could*
anything that she had said or done have helped
to bring this about ? There was nothing that
she could remember—nothing at all, except
that Josy had asked her, in the little moment
when they had been following Miss Heriot
and Dally up the hill, whether anything was

wrong, and whether she might help. " I don't think—" began Sally through dry lips.

" Sara and Josy were both with me all the time, Miss Dean." Miss Heriot, seeing the white look on Sally's face, spoke up. " Josy seemed quite cheery and like herself during that part of the day. It was while we were coming home that I noticed she seemed quiet and very tired."

" Who, then, was with Josy during the day ? " Miss Dean's question followed at once.

A number of replies followed, more or less in chorus, from members of the various parties which Josy had joined. The various mistresses concerned made method of the muddlesome material thus offered.

" Josy, then, was with her own form until lunch-time ? Thank you, Daphne." Miss Dean took down notes. " Finding fuel for the fire. Yes. After lunch, on the strawberry hill with the rest. That accounts for most of the time. Who was with Josy after tea ? "

There was a pause.

" Miss Dean "—it was Hilary's voice—" me it was. We'd meant to, anyway. She wanted to go to the Wishing Pool. That was all." Hilary's voice was shaky. " Only——"

" Only ? Yes, my dear. You went with her ? "

" I wanted to, Miss Dean. Truly, I did. And we'd meant to wish together. But she'd changed her wish between starting and getting there. And—" Hilary's voice was still more shaky.

" Yes, my dear. Take your time, and think before you speak."

" Well, then, she would go in alone. She went there while I was helping Miss Heriot catch Dally, or I'd have been there too; only not inside, because, though she really funked rather, she said she'd *have* to go alone because it was a secret wish." Hilary stopped.

" Then she was alone in the grotto, you say, Hilary ? " Miss Dean was looking very intently.

" Oh yes, quite, Miss Heriot, except—" Hilary stopped for a moment. " She did say " —Hilary's tone sounded as though she was suddenly remembering—" that she'd seen a gipsy there. A woman who was a perfectly nice gipsy, she said, and a kind of friend of hers, and——"

" Hilary, you may come to my room and tell the rest of your story there," said Miss Dean's quiet voice. " Miss Heriot, will you kindly take roll for me, and then the girls may go upstairs."

Upstairs, with everybody's tongue loosed as

soon as the hall was left, with everybody whispering in awed voices, with everybody looking questioningly at each other ; everybody except Sally—*her* one and only desire was to be left alone.

   *   *   *   *   *

" If a chap just knew—" Perry was lying flat on his back in his bed in the dorm. Pollitt was snoring the snore of the just in the next one. " If a chap jolly well could just get at the root of it, but—well, under the circs., he jolly well *can't !* I've simply got to keep on keeping on. Though how Joe Hinnigan gets into it, too, I cannot tumble to. It's a rotten affair, and he and I seem in the same boat—at least, he's jolly well worse off than I am *yet*. Still, any old way under the circs.—" Perry carefully lowered his head under the blankets and, by the light of an electric torch, proceeded to investigate a strip of paper.

" Under the circs., owing to this, I jolly well *can't*, for the sake of Beeches, do any other thing than I jolly well *am* doing, even if " —Perry's head remained under the blankets, though his electric torch light had been extinguished —" even—if—Beeches—kicks—me— out."

CHAPTER XXVIII

SALLY GUESSES AND—GOES

SALLY knew what she was going to do. She was going after Josy, of course. Since Hilary's statement in hall she had suddenly understood, or had thought she understood. Josy must have met their gipsy woman, and she had, for some reason, gone to the camp. There had been whispered rumours in the dorm., of course, but Sally, listening silently, had contributed no word to the conversation.

" The gipsies. Evidently Miss Dean thinks it must be the gipsies. They've jolly well taken her." Thus Hesther and Dorothy.

" You utter loonies." Thus Sheila. " Anybody'd think you lived in the days of Queen Victoria. Josy kidnapped, is it? Pish! Buck up and get into bed, if you haven't anything more sensible to say. If, as Hilary says, it was one of our dorm. gipsies, the broomselling ones, why, they've camped round about here for years, and nobody's found much fault with them yet. They're absolutely all right."

" Well, anyhow, somebody said that the police were going to move *all* the gipsies on from the Downs this year, so you needn't—" Nobody likes to be labelled as Victorian nowadays. Hesther and Dorothy were no exception to the rule, as their stately tones expressed.

" Well, that's simply because of those rotten notes, and all the fairs and things. It's not that they suspect the gipsies. I'd like to see a gipsy making counterfeit notes ! " remarked Sheila.

" Oh, well "—Hesther and Dorothy subsided. Everybody got into bed, and, though feeling horribly anxious, went to sleep. For talk in the dorms., having dealt with the Josy subject as thoroughly as it could, dropped away into nothingness. Nobody wanted to air spook tales and talk of ghosty things to-night just because—just because twelve-year-old Josy, the child who not many nights ago had bravely owned to the rest in that very dorm. how much she sympathized with Mary's fears herself, was, perhaps, out in the open in smugglers' country somewhere to-night. It was a relief to feel sure, since the best thing they could do to help, as Miss Heriot had pointed out, was to keep rules and behave ordinarily without fuss, that nothing would be left undone by Miss Dean which should be done, and that before morning surely Josy must certainly be found.

None of them would sleep, however, they were certain of that. The events of the day's holidaying seemed to the girls as though they had all happened long, long ago. Even although their feet still ached and tingled, the girls yet felt that the dance could not possibly have been in full swing such a short time since. None of them would sleep, they were certain of that.

But, in spite of their assurances to each other, the Down air was already working its magic, and the unwonted exercise of the day had laid its spell. In half an hour three girls, at least, in Josy's dorm. were fast locked in their deepest dreams. Every girl except Sally. And Sally was far too unhappy to sleep. She was waiting, waiting till she knew herself unnoticed, then she would slip out. At first she had made up her mind, just as soon as Hilary's words had died away in hall, that she would go straight to Miss Dean. She had even got so far as to approach Miss Heriot with a mumbled request to speak to the Head.

" But, Sara "—Miss Heriot listened carefully, but her eyes looked surprised—" when Miss Dean asked you *particularly*, you said——"

"Yes, Miss Heriot. But now I think that perhaps——"

"Sara, is it anything really definite? You will understand, just as well as I do, that time matters just now very much indeed. Miss Dean is most anxious for real help; but if it is only to be a string of conjectures and 'perhapses' which will lead us nowhere——"

Sally realized suddenly what a rigmarole the story *would* be that she would have to tell; what a "string of conjectures and perhapses" it would be, indeed, that story which must go back, back, back to the very first day of term, if she were to explain everything to the Head. The story which, she realized now, she ought to have told long ago. And suppose, suppose at the end of it, Miss Dean should not credit it? Suppose Miss Dean should even forbid Sally to follow up her idea? The girl went back to her line without a word and walked upstairs, only half-hearing the whispered talk all round her on the subject of the night. But Sally had by no means given up her conviction on account of Miss Heriot's words. She meant to work on it by herself, that was all. As soon as the sound of Sheila's steady breathing had added itself to the chorus from the beds of Hesther and Dorothy, she knew that it was safe to go.

Out of the window; it was perfectly easy. Sally had quite forgotten rules. For weeks now she had managed to keep them; she had felt the spell of Beech Trees weaving itself round her deliciously; and she had been happy—at least, she could have been happy but for the gloomy foreboding that some ill might come still by means of the letter which the gipsies held. She could have been happy, in just the same way as other girls at Beech Trees were happy, just *because* she was one of them. But to-night Beech Trees itself was forgotten; everything was forgotten save one certainty which gripped at Sally's heart—that Josy was somewhere out on the moor; that Josy had gone to the camp; that she had found out through the gipsies the secret which Sally had tried to hide from her, and that she had gone, in spite of the spooks that she dreaded, in spite of the fact that to break the traditions of Beech Trees was, to Josy, like breaking off a piece of her heart, to fetch Sally's letter back.

" They've probably asked her for money like they did me; and so she realized, poor kid," thought Sally as she ran, " that they'd got it still. She thinks it's her fault that the letter ever got into their hands, and it's my beastly, beastly fault that she thinks so. Oh, it's *all* my beastly fault ! "

Sally had raced over the school field by this time; she was taking, though she didn't know it, very much the same way that Josy had taken an hour or two before. She was still thinking, thinking, as she reached the Down path and ran quickly towards the camp.

As Josy had gone it had taken all her courage to force down the fears which would crowd round her—fears of night, and silly terrors which, although she knew them to be silly and groundless, she could not quite push away. She had noticed every ripple of a grass tuft, every rustle of a bush, every pad-pad of a rabbit's foot, every pee-wit of a sudden plover, and the whole of her palpitating, beating heart had been given up to trying to be as brave as she ought to be so that she could reach the camp in time.

As Sally went, her thoughts were different, quite. She didn't care in the very least for darkness; she hardly noticed it. The chilly breath of night-time only served to nerve her up as she ran. The sounds and scents of evening gave her no sudden thrills of apprehension, for she scarcely realized them. Spooks were truly nothing to Sally, for she didn't care. But as she went her thoughts flew back and back.

It might all have been so easily prevented, all this, if she'd not made such an ass of herself by trying to pretend—trying to impress the rest, trying to seem wonderful. Even Josy, who had stood by her right through, and who was standing by her now (Sally gave a gulp), had said, really, from the beginning that that first day's happening didn't much matter, and that *any* one of the girls might have met with the experience which to Sally had seemed so terribly demeaning.

But Sally hadn't wanted to be just " anybody " then. She must be a law unto herself, and it was because of that that all her troubles had started—the troubles which had involved others besides herself, and which seemed growing greater instead of less. The letter to Perry, posted by pigeon-post against rules ! Oh, if Josy had suggested the method, it was only because of Sally's foolish fear.

The other rules that Sally had broken, just to show, in case Sybil might find the matter out, that she really wasn't such a fool as she might have appeared. The runaway canter and its effects on Josy ! The reappearance of the gipsies with their threatenings which still hung over her head like Damocles' sword ! Then the rumour about Perry's disgrace, which, being connected in some strange way with pigeons and letters, Sally couldn't help feeling was somehow muddled up with everything else !

And now, after a lull, during which Sally had hoped that there would be no more trouble, quite suddenly this, which might be worse than anything ; what *was* worse, to Sally, than anything that had happened before. Because now Josy was alone, nobody knew where ; Josy, the timidly-courageous, without Sally, the daring, who didn't care.

But suddenly Sally realized that she *did* care. Things had happened with her, as Miss Dean had said they would. There was something for whom Sally cared and that was—Josy. Life—she remembered the Head's words—could never be quite so simple again now. It had begun—the caring—in the Puck-the-pony way, as Sally called it to herself. It had gone on growing all the time, but more than ever while Josy was ill. It had grown and grown, because of Josy's sportingness and courage, until she had realized since half-term that she wouldn't have Josy taking half-blame any more. It was for that reason Sally had held aloof from Josy ; but Josy's will had beaten hers.

" She's braver than I am, and bigger, though she's smaller, in everything that matters ; and stronger though she's frightened," thought Sally as she ran. " It all began because I'm a miserable, despicable coward. I kept saying that I didn't mind, and thinking it, but all the while I minded most horribly what the girls thought of me, and that is just why it began."

Sally gave a half sob. Then she pulled herself up. She had faced things ; she knew herself better than she had ever known herself before. But she wasn't going to give in under the knowledge ; she had Josy to find. It was just after this that she reached the gorse clump which hid the entrance to the Hidden Ways.

She had come up cautiously in the semi-darkness, wondering if she might meet the gipsies on the way. She had not expected, in spite of the fact that the rumour of the camp moving had already reached Beech Trees, to find the site a desolate one. Sally, as she stood in the darkness, holding back the branches so that the dim light should shine in, felt her heart suddenly throb with fear.

For where was Josy ? Had she been here ? Was she gone again, or had she never come ? Was Sally's quest fruitless ? The gipsies had gone ; and was Josy with them ? Or had she never come this way at all ?

On either side of her stretched the hollow pathway, leading underground in one direction towards the sea entrance used in past gone years by the smugglers with their spoils. In the other direction the Hidden Ways might stretch for miles and miles, with few or many entrances from the Down for all she knew, but with a main exit, so Miss Heriot had said, opening out somewhere on the other side of the hills.

Was it any good going on ?   Should she go back to Beech Trees again ?

It was just as she was deliberating that her quick ears caught the sound of voices—voices talking quickly and eagerly not far away. The speakers were evidently lying low near by among the bushes screening the Hidden Ways. Sally slipped a little deeper into the sunken roadway and cowered there, listening eagerly. Perhaps she might gain some clue as to Josy's whereabouts.

CHAPTER XXIX

WHAT SALLY HEARD

" AH, sure, 'twill be safely hid; 'tis Bina's took it."

It was the voice of the gipsy man. Sally recognized it at once.

" Took it, eh? Bina? Then you've upped and tell't her of it, then?" The answering voice sounded half-uneasy. Evidently the speaker had only just arrived; his words came rather breathlessly as though he had been running, and it seemed likely that he had approached the spot from the seaward end of the Hidden Ways.

" Gipsies have sharp ears; they'd have heard me, but for the fact that he was on the way too," thought Sally, listening still. " Did he pass Josy as he came? If so, he'll speak of her. If not, she won't have gone that way; and so if she's in the Hidden Ways at all I shall be safe to explore along this end." She crouched very still, and the voices went on.

" We's ready for flitting ; the van's ready.
All your stuff's up along o' ours. And Trillia's
wanting Bina to know as the baby's sleeping
sweet."

There was a change in the answering voice.
" Ah, sure the baby 'll mend now. And Bina
will hearten up w'en she's a-done what she's
off to do. The luck's changed. I've given my
word to wait on her here while she's a-hiding
of it. Wouldn't rest, Bina wouldn't, till it
was done. Then we'll come along, Palermo,
sure. No, Bina never knew nought at all of
the matter, Bina didn't, not till yesterday night.
Then the chye being took grievous ill and all,
she was that un-comeable that I'd got to tell her.
A witching bird, so she said, she'd seen, Bina
did ; a-chattering round it was and meaning us
to move on, for trouble would come. Taking
on so, Bina was, with the baby ill and all, and
her always sure as sure that a-holding back of
that letter had brought black luck for the baby.
Well, then, I'd just to tell her that the black
luck wasn't from that at all, but from something
mighty different and all."

" You tell't her of the notes, Manfrey, and
the pollis ? "

" Well, and why for not? She'd got to
know. And what with the last trick of all the
rye played us two weeks past, sending back

that onlucky packet in her basket last time she
went! Sure, all the while Bina never knew
nothing at all when she were fetching and
carrying of them notes. Jest to the rye's
house she'd to go with her brooms every week,
and ask the rawnee there for a meal. That was
what the arrangement was, sure, with the rye.
Fixed it up, we did, outside the ' Plough and
Horses ' at Pyecombe, him and me and you,
you'll remember, Palermo. ' Don't yer go
drookering and bringing down the eyes of the
pollis on yer, Bina,' ses I. ' Jest take what they
gives you thankful at the rye's house and don't
arsk nothin' more, an' that's all. There's
money to it, Bina,' ses I, ' and wealth an' riches
for the baby.' And she does it, Bina does. An'
the notes come that way to us, as yer knows,
Palermo, and we passed 'em fine at the fairs.
Paid up, too, the rye did, fair and pleasant in
the first ; but 'twas a low-down trick what he
played at the last."

" Ay, and bunked he did. House were
shut up last time I were that way. Hartist
he called himself, and a rye without work he
were. Ay, but it were a right-down low
trick."

" You knows. 'Tis two weeks back now.
There'd been kind of rumours that the pollis
was at the fairs, and when Bina calls as usual

and waits, out comes the rawnee with a smile
—too sweet to be pleasant 'er smile was that
day, so Bina says—and a packet of 'extrys,'
as she says. And Bina takes it all unknowing.
Well, if it weren't a reg'lar boree-hokanee
trick! The pollis was after them, that's sure
what they feared, and they'd palmered off the
whole box o' tricks on Bina, and she'd, all unknowing, to bring it back to camp. Weighed
heavy on 'er it did all daytime. There was a
sort of a something onnatural about it, Bina
says, there was. Well, and when I opens of it
at night there wasn't no notes at all. No pay-
money, neither, for the last lot. Nothing but
that there trick-box fer making of them,
palmered off on us poor Romany folk!"

"I reckon it put Bina out a bit to hear it
all larst night," put in the voice.

"'Twas me wot got put out first, I tell
you. Bina didn't know naught at all for a fair
fortnight. Hid the box in the camp, I did,
at first, not being knowledgeable of what to do
with it. And then—well, I ups and does something what Bina swears is what brought the
black luck on the baby." Manfrey's voice
sounded shamefaced. "I'd a whole heap of
them false notes over and above what I'd
palmed off at the fair, and didn't know what
on earth to do rightly with 'em, for fear of the

pollis. And it took my mind sudden like magic
that it might clear blame off we poor Romanies,
what never meant ill to nobody but just to
make wealth for the work we'd to do, if I paid
'em on unbeknownst to some un who'd get
out of it luckier than we. There was a matter
of a few o' them carrying-pigeons flying atween
Hinnigan's below there and the Beeches school
of young gents. Well, I'd, unbeknownst,
stopped one of 'em oncest—we having no
manner of notion that they wasn't wild ones
meant for Romany food, like; and there was a
letter "—the voice was lowered. " Bina says
. . . five shilluns . . . proud, haughty rawnee."
The whispers were low, and then grew clearer
again.

" 'Twas all beknownst to Bina, then, I lays
hold on the next pigeon I sees flying, and
fastens a note, easy-like, under its wings. I
does that again, and more than once. 'Twas
a matter of two weeks ago, and the box o'
tricks having been palmered off on me by the
rye I didn't much care how I got rid of 'em.
An easy-like way I thought it. ' The rye wot
gets them will part with them pretty quick,'
thinks I, ' and the Romanies won't be blamed.' "

" Eh, Manfrey ? " The other was evidently
listening as eagerly as was Sally.

" ' Eh ! '—yes, it *were* ' Eh ! ' " Manfrey spat

into the fern. "For then there comes news as that Hinnigan's been took off. Notes found in the 'Cosy,' there—well, like enough there were! For you, Palermo, yer own self, was the Romany wot brought this grye and pays him in ten o' them notes; you'll not be denying of it."

"No, no. And I'd no manner of feelin' against Hinnigan. Ef he'd only set to and bought another rye that fair day he'd have passed the notes easy-come-go; it wasn't much gain I got to myself at all, but——"

"You're right. But what with them notes being found down in 'Cosy,' and what wi' the notes the pigeons had took, the blame fair got nailed down on Joe. And it weren't fair. I weren't saying naught to Bina, but with that there trick-box dumped here so onnatural in camp, I didn't know rightly what to do for the best. Romanies don't never act bad to a kind heart, and Joe, there, had always been mighty feeling in his ways to we afore they took him. 'Well,' ses I, 'there's others as ain't so feeling-like as what Joe is.' And then I minds me of that there letter wot I tells you of, Palermo. 'Ryes and rawnees gets out of troubles sooner ever than what we Romanies does,' thinks I, wise, 'and 'twill surely help Joe, as well as we, if I does it,' ses I. Well, then, so I *does* it. The letter was all writ of secrets and such-like, and signed by the rawnee's own hand. Well, so I sends it with the last of them false notes by one of them pigeons." Manfrey stopped.

Sally's breath came in such deep, long gasps that she was almost afraid the speakers would detect her presence, but after a while Manfrey went on,—

" But, happen, seems the blame didn't get shifted. Happen, seems it ain't done Joe nothing of good that I knows on. There haven't been no word of that there letter since then, and Joe still lays in jail. Well, and luck seemed took from us, too, straight away ; and when the baby took ill and all, and Bina fair beside herself, and neither to hold nor yet to bind in her talk last night, as you may say, well, I up and told her. Showed her the onnatural trick-box, too, what had got palmered off on us, and arsted her 'pinion. Bina's 'pinion's worth getting, it is, and what with the pollis talking of shifting our camps, and p'r'aps coming here and finding of that trick-box, I just couldn't think of no not-to-say securesome hiding-place, the luck being always turning against us. Well, Bina had her mind made up so soon as she'd set eyes on it."

" Eh ? " The listener spoke eagerly.

" ' Dump un in Wishing Pool,' ses Bina. That were why she brought the baby over to Trillia this morning. But when she reaches Wishing Pool, what would she find there but all the rawnees from the big school. Laughing and gay they was, Bina says, and she fair distraught with the baby ill down at Trillia's van and her with the trick-box hid in her skirt! Well, and hide it she couldn't, Bina says, what with the rawnees all laughing and saying that there weren't no magic in the Pool and that it weren't bottomless, nor ghosty, nor nothing, and talking so onnatural-like, they was, that Bina shook to hear 'em. For all *she* knowed, says Bina, one or other of 'em might put their hands in and draw it out ef she hid it there. Well, an' wen they'd gone their ways from the Pool, she decides that she'll just give a wish for the baby, and then come away with the onlucky box, an' hide it somewheres else." Manfrey stopped.

" An' she did, eh? Sure, the baby picked up something wonderful, Trillia says, just about sundown," put in the other.

" She did go for to wish, sure. But it seems like as though the black luck weren't leaving of us." Manfrey's voice sounded dejected. " There was a rawnee, a small rawnee wot Bina's took an uncommon liking for—her what came here before-times with the proud rawnee, like I've said. Well, 'twere she came on Bina as she were a-wishing there, and sobbing for the baby something fearful ; and being not on-natural-inclined, like what the other clever rawnees are and laughing at magic, she gave a wish for the baby too. And she did it, Bina will persist, in a kind of exchange-sort-of-like for that there letter wot I told you of. 'Here, now,' says Bina, when she gets back, and me only just home from the fair at Plashett; 'here, then,' says she, very uppersome, 'I wants that there letter, and no five shilluns more for it, neither, for you've got better un that, since the baby's picked up wonderful at sundown, Trillia says '—her having looked in on Trillia on the way home, Palermo. And then she tells me, still uppersome, of the little rawnee what wished in the Pool. 'Now, Bina,' I ses, 'I can't noways do it, for I ain't got no letter ; not for five shilluns or five pounds neither,' I ses. And then I telled her that part of the story which I hadn't telled her before. And I thought she'd take on to the death of her. For the rawnee was coming, so she says, to fetch un. And she'd a-sooner lose the heart in her breast than disappoint the rawnee. Coming at sundown, so Bina said as she was, to fetch the letter. 'Well'"—Manfrey's voice sounded sulky—"''tisn't as though you's even got quit of the box for all your high-sounding words of promises,' I ses to her, upbraiding-like. ' 'Tis the box what brings the black luck, and not no nonsense about what I done with no letter. And now you arsks the rawnee to come, and me with no letter. And next thing 'twill be the pollis for that there box,' I ses, ' and me in jail.' "

" Ay."

" Well, then, Bina ups, her eyes all flashing. ' And that there box will be hid—proper hid,' she ses, with her blood up. ' And hid where none will find it, and you not put in jail,' ses Bina. ' And all wot *you* got to do,' ses Bina, ' is jest to wait here, and when the rawnee comes you can be telling her to wait for me, and that I'll be back and tell her truth about that there letter,' ses Bina. ' And that will I.' And off she goes."

" Eh, but where will she be hiding of it ? " broke in Palermo.

There came a whisper, followed by exclamations of amazement.

" Sure, Bina'd never go there ! 'Tis an onnatural-like place," said Palermo.

" Sure, but she will. 'Tis to take black luck off us." Manfrey's voice was proud. " An' soon as she's back-along, Palermo, we'll be coming over to you. We've got naught here now that isn't loaded up with your stuff, and we'll be off in next county before the pollis thinks of moving us."

"But the rawnee? Did she come?" The voices sounded more distant.

"She'll not be a-coming. Bina's been gone this hour, and she'll be back sure, soon. Yes, she bade me wait for the rawnee; but I hasn't heard no sign nor steps." Manfrey's voice was sly. "Maybe I've been a wee way off laying snares for a rabbit or two; but I'll be able to tell Bina that the rawnee never kept no appointingment, and that there weren't nothing for her to explain to the rawnee because the rawnee never come that *I* see! Well, and to-morrow we'll be off, Palermo, and that should bring settlement, sure, to Bina's mind."

CHAPTER XXX

A PASSAGE PERILOUS

SALLY had gained much information during her silent vigil. As the voices ceased she sat staring incredulously into the darkness for a moment or two. She could hardly believe that she had understood aright. It *was* the gipsies, then, who had been passing the notes; and yet, as she realized, they had been, in a way, more sinned against than sinning. Joe Hinnigan, clearly, was not to blame, and the gipsies knew that, and it had been in trying to help Joe, in their strange gipsy way, that the letter had been sent by pigeon-post after all to Perry at school. This, then, surely must be at the root, somehow, of Perry's disgrace. But all these things must wait. Sally had no heart for anything else just now but Josy—Josy, who was still to find.

Had she come this way? Sally had gained enough insight into the gipsy man's character through listening to his talk to realize that he had evidently made up his mind that he would *not* hear her, should she come, if he could help it. He wanted to save the situation by pretending to Bina, who had certainly made up her mind that Josy should know the truth, that the child had not kept her appointment after all.

But if Josy had said she was coming she *would* come, Sally knew. Josy, then, had been to the camp—Sally was certain of that. But, seeing the signs of flitting, had the child returned home ? Had she and Sally passed close to each other on the Down ? or had she in some way divined—what Sally knew from listening to the Romany talk—that Bina was away on a secret errand to some spot in the Hidden Ways—some spot so " onnatural " that the men could only speak of it with bated breath in frightened whispers ? If so, Sally was going after her. If there was the merest bit of likelihood that Josy had gone, Sally meant to follow. For what strange, uncanny dangers might not lie in the direction which, having listened to the men's talk, Sally knew that they themselves would not have dared to take !

Even Sally, as she crouched in the Hidden Ways, with darkness to right of her, darkness to left of her, but with only one course ahead of her to follow, just in case Josy, the timidly-courageous, should be there, felt a qualm such as Childe Roland might have felt on his way to the dark tower. But the feeling of fear was not so much for herself as for Josy—Josy, who might be ahead. It was as she realized this that Sally raised herself from her crouching position on the bank and groped along the sunken roadway.

It was pitch dark; it was narrow; on either side, if she stretched her arms widely, she could feel the banks which towered up over her head. Even now and then in the darkness branches from left or right, from above her—sometimes even, so it seemed, from below—touched her face with unseen ghostly hands. Brambles tore at her skirts; the uneven ground hurt her feet; no light whatever filtered in through the thick tangled growth which surmounted the towering banks on either side. At midday the shadowy gloom might have been pleasant, perhaps; at night, however, the Hidden Ways seemed a very nightmare of a place, leading, as Sally had heard the gipsies say, to some spot so terrible that no one would dare to go there. For that reason the coiner's trick-box might lie there safe and sound.

No one but Bina at least! For the baby's sake she was facing horrors which must have been dreadful to her, to take the black luck away.

No one but Josy, who was following Bina, Sally somehow felt sure, with Sally's own interests keeping terror from her twelve-year-old heart !

No one but Sally (though Sally didn't realize that she made a third in the brave little band), who was beating down fears which were not the less because this was the first time in all her daring life that Sally *had* been afraid in just this way !

On went Sally ; where, she did not know. It might be miles and miles before the Hidden Ways opened out on the other side of the Down. There might be chance openings before then, through the banks, of course, but she meant to struggle on until Josy should be found. At first walking upright she went, feeling with her hands ; then crouching to avoid the slashing branches ; then crawling on hands and knees in weariness.

How far she had gone Sally did not know, and how long she had taken over her passage perilous she had no idea, when at last she waited for a little to rest and regain her breath. With every pain and ache she realized, somehow, that Josy, far smaller and weaker but very brave, was bearing them too. For her sake, for Sally's sake, Josy was bearing them, just as Sally was glad to bear them for Josy. If she could find the child and bring her home, that was all Sally asked. Everything in the world seemed dwarfed almost to nothingness by the immensity of her longing to reach Josy.

It was at that moment, as she crouched and thought, that she heard a sound not far away —a little, breathless sound; the sound as of some one sighing who could hardly gasp out the sigh; then the sound of some one trying to pipe up a weak little song. Sally suddenly crouched down again, taut and tense with amazement. For one minute thoughts of ghostly presences seemed almost real as she listened, then—

> " Bathing in a dew-pond
> Is the greatest fun,"

came the little gasping singing voice.

It was Josy! Who else *could* it be? Josy singing to try and keep herself brave! The last time Sally had heard that song it had been sung by Josy, clad in pyjamas, dancing a two-step on her bed in the dorm. But now—

> " But not till the chill is off . . ."

The voice shook and died away as Sally moved again.

" Josy, it's me ! " said Sally.

She found Josy in her arms then — Josy, shaking and shivering, and quivering and quaking, but still brave. Sally could feel Josy's heart beating with big hard thumps against her own. Sally could hear Josy's voice speaking in a husky whisper which tried to be a welcoming shout.

" Sally ! Sally ! Sally ! "

In answer, Sally, for the first time in her life, pressed her warm red lips to Josy's cold little cheek, and held the child close. " Josy darling ! Oh, Josy darling ! " Sally had never known that she had it in her to feel as she did. The spooks of the Hidden Ways were forgotten ; everything was forgotten except that she held Josy close, and that she would never let her go.

" Sally, you're not a dream, are you ? You followed me ? But however—" Josy was whispering a little less breathlessly now, but she was still holding fast to Sally with a grip of terror, although she did not know it. Her muscles were taut and tense ; she was panting still. " I came. You see, I just thought I would come. The gipsy woman had promised me your letter, Sally, so I just came to fetch it. I didn't think it would be so far ; but when I came to the camp they'd moved on, you see, and I wouldn't have known what to do but for the patrin."

" The ' patrin ' ? "

" She'd left it—for me, of course. She'd left little bunches of heather. There was one close to the fire ashes, arranged pointing this way, like Miss Heriot told us. She'd promised faithfully to give me the letter, so I knew I was meant to follow on. But after I'd seen two or three of them the light went, you see, and I couldn't follow easily any longer. And I thought I'd got lost, and then—" Josy's voice, which had sounded bravely chirpy to begin with, trailed off.

" It's all right, Josy." Sally's arms were round her. " I know everything. And the letter's all right. I'll tell you later on. Were you resting here when you sang ? " She was saying anything, with her lips pressed to Josy's hair ; just talking nothings until Josy's heart should beat less wildly.

" I sang because I was funking, I think ; not to remember that I was, you know. And because I was too tired to go on. And "— Josy's voice sank still lower—" because there are the queerest, spookiest noises going on quite close here, Sally."

" Rot," said Sally, trying to revert to her usual breezy tone. " I made the ' spooky

noises,' I expect, coming along on all-fours like
a centipede."

"Yes, perhaps. Some of them. But there
were others closer, and this side of us, Sally.
Listen."

Together the girls sat deep in the bushes
and held their breath. Then suddenly Sally
realized that Josy was right. There *were* queer,
rustling noises near at hand, only she hadn't
noticed them because her thoughts had been
given entirely to the child at her side. Now
she *did* hear.

It was, as Josy had said, eerie and queer—
like a quick moving, like a rustling, like the
half-wild movements of some terrified thing
trying to make up its mind to escape. Then
suddenly, while they listened breathlessly, like
a dark streak a figure seemed to shoot past
them in the darkness of the Hidden Ways from
the spot where the sounds had seemed to come.

"O-o-oh!" In spite of herself a terrified
whisper broke from Josy.

"*Josy!*" Sally seized her hand. "Josy!
buck up! It's not a ghost. How could it
be? It's somebody who's been frightened of *us*,
I believe—our whisperings and your singing.
Somebody who thought *us* spooks! It's just
somebody who must have been waiting at one
of the openings on to the Down. If we **go**

through that way ourselves, why, we'll perhaps get out on to the open at once." As she whispered Sally hurried the child towards the spot from which the flying figure had come. " *Why !* " cried Sally then.

CHAPTER XXXI

CLANG-G ! CLANG-G-G ! CLANG-G-G-G !

FOR they found themselves in a large open space, so dark that they could not tell what were their surroundings except insomuch as they knew that they were free from the encompassing bushes and briars and brambles of the Hidden Ways. They were not in the Hidden Ways, it seemed, any longer. They had crept through a smallish opening by which the terrified figure whom they had seen had escaped. That was all they knew.

" We're somewhere, anyhow," Sally was beginning when—

Crash ! Something banged to behind them. Sally turned like a dart in the darkness, then felt her way with her hands towards the opening through which they had crept. It was closed ! Where were they ? Was this magic indeed ? For how could a chamber like this open out from the banks of the Hidden Ways? How could such a thing be possible ? But it *had*

happened ! And something else happened.
Suddenly a voice high with terror, almost
banshee-like, was heard calling from outside.

" And 'twas for the good luck, sure, that I
laid down the patrin in my fearsomeness !
But the black luck it is as has followed me.
Ah, stay there, then, will you, in your fearful-
ness, and leave the poor wee Romany baby
free ! "

" It's the gipsy woman," faltered Josy.

" It's Bina," said Sally.

Together they hammered at the chamber
door, but no reply came. If the gipsy heard
them, she was far too terrified to know who
they were, or to care to find out. Their
very shouts, as they realized, would only drive
her the more hastily away.

" Where are we ? " asked Josy.

Sally had no idea. Dread terror was grip-
ping her—the girl who did not care ; dread
terror that they might be shut up here for ever,
in this strangest of hiding-places in the Hidden
Ways. Some niche it must be, Sally told herself, known only to the old-time smugglers
and the gipsies ; some place which every one
dreaded—so the men had said ; some place—
Sally's thoughts were switched off at the sound
of Josy's voice.

" Sally, it's most awfully breathlessy here."

It was. There had been air in the Hidden
Ways; though the bushes were thickly matted
overhead, yet there had been air to breathe
there. Here they must be right under the
Down—in a kind of tunnel, was it? The
place felt chill and damp, and airless too.

" Here, it's partly tiredness, kid. Lie down
for a bit on my coat. You'll get your breath
back," said Sally, taking command. For, with
a sudden, panting realization, she had understood where they were — what this place was
with its cold, damp smell. And Josy must not
know! The walls of their prison were stone;
the ground on which they stood was cold:
they were under the Down. It must be—
Sally knew that the way they had taken ran due
east—near the church. Their prison was an
empty tomb! They were, Sally felt suddenly
sure, in the Haunted Tomb, near which no
villager dare go.

So *this* was the smugglers' secret, was it?
The girls had said that all the village ghosts
were made up by the smugglers, and so the
Haunted Tomb had never been a real tomb
at all—just a dumping ground for smuggled
goods. Bina had known; and she had decided,
terror or not terror, to hide the trick-box
here where it would be safe. Then—so Sally
pieced things together—it was likely that she

should be terrified to hear whisperings and
faint singings when she was engaged in hiding
the box. She had been too terrified at first
to come out, fearing to meet some awful spooky
presence lying in wait; but having made up
her mind suddenly to rush past, she had, on
seeing the supposed spooks enter the vault
which she had left, plucked up courage, for
the baby's sake, to bang the door on them
fast " to imprison the black luck ! "

" If that's what's happened, as I believe,"
thought Sally, " the ' trick-box ' will be here.
When Josy's asleep, I'll go round on hands
and knees and find it, and then—well, I'll be
sure."

It wasn't long before Josy slept. Stretched
out on Sally's coat on the floor of the Haunted
Tomb she dreamed dreams of safety and peace
while Sally went her rounds.

On hands and knees, inch by inch. The box
would be in some corner. Well, when she found
it, clue though it was, what good would the
clue be to them ? Sally asked herself. She
knew enough already to exonerate Joe and
Mary from all blame ; she knew nearly enough
to explain Perry's disgrace. She had her own
story to tell, too, back, back, and back, right
to the beginning ; for it was she herself who
had brought nearly all the trouble, she thought.

But how, and when? They might never get out.

" *Ah !* "

It was so sudden; it was quite unexpected. And then so wonderful! There was the edge of the trick-box; she felt it suddenly. Then, as her hands groped around it, they suddenly turned cold, as Sally's heart gave a loud, sudden throb and then seemed to stop. For, close by, there seemed to be the edge of a door, set in the side of the vault, with a metal ring. Sally pulled at the metal ring with desperate strength, and it creaked slowly back.

" Josy ! " Sally could hardly breathe the whisper. But Josy still slept. " I'll go alone, then," said Sally to herself. " Suppose it's *not* a way of release ! "

But it was. Right under the floor of the belfry of the little church the trap-door opened— the church where the Beech Treesites sat every Sunday, the church where Sally and Josy, sitting in the school pew, had thought their long, long thoughts that first Sunday before the runaway canter over the Down. So long ago it seemed; so much had happened since then. A lamp was burning over the altar. By its faint light Sally realized, after a while, where she was. Josy was safe.

It was in the Beech Trees pew now, while

Josy still slept, that Sally broke down and sobbed as she had never sobbed before, and shed tears that meant to her more than anything had ever meant before. It was after that that she decided what to do.

The church was locked. There was no way of release till morning, but one. Up the belfry steps went Sally, and with all the strength of her arms she pulled the rope of the single bell.

Clang-g-g-g !

And as she rang the thought came to her of that very first Saturday of all, when she had rung another bell—the Beech Trees fire-bell. And as she rang with all her might, she felt that somehow, up in the little church belfry, she was ringing out the Sally-who-hadn't-really-been-Sally-at-all, and ringing in the new-and-worth-while Sally, who would somehow be better worthy of Beech Trees now.

Clang-g ! Clang-g-g ! Clang-g-g-g !

*   *   *   *   *

Down at the church cottage the verger roused himself anxiously and hurriedly felt for his keys.

*   *   *   *   *

Josy, in the Haunted Tomb, still sleeping, stirred for one moment to murmur Sally's name before she dropped off again to the sound of the bell and dreamed of school.

*   *   *   *   *

Up at Beech Trees mistresses and girls awakened, and the same thought came to each of them at the sound, " The lost girls—could it possibly be ? "

* * * * *

At The Beeches, Perry, sleeping none too well during the last few weeks, was awakened, too, by the clanging far away. And not realizing exactly what it was that had roused him, he groped, as usual, for the slip of paper and read it again under the blankets by the aid of the electric torch : " *Please keep my secret and don't mention it to any one.—Sara Heath*." Pinned to the slip was a false treasury note ! " Well, it's no good making bones about it," sighed Perry, " it's got to be seen through. Keep a stiff upper lip, of course ; that's all a chap can do ! And who jolly well knows," he turned over drowsily, " things *may* turn up trumps all right, like they always do to the chaps in books ! "

THE END